The Facts
Behind
the
Helsinki
Roccamatios

"Martel has a storytelling brain. He's not afraid of improbability, and he sees metaphors everywhere ... Martel's charm, here and in *Life of Pi,* has much to do with the paradoxical honesty of the plainly fictional ... Entirely delightful." —*The New York Times Book Review*

"Martel's slip of a book contains just four of his pre–*Life of Pi* stories, but they pack a powerful punch ... With uncommon dexterity, Martel manages to inject real, poignant feeling into cleverly conceived experimental fictions." —*Entertainment Weekly*

"*The Facts* ... represents the best reason we've been given yet to keep reading Martel." —*Kirkus Reviews*

"Martel chooses not to repeat himself, here offering four meditative stories that test the limits of the form ... Elusive and thought-provoking." —*Library Journal*

"With formats ranging from conventional to inventive, all the stories in *The Facts Behind the Helsinki Roccamatios* not only entertain but erupt with emotional notes that surprise ... Martel's clean, unsullied prose is packed with power. He fills the theater of the mind with bright notes that resonate long after the curtain closes." —*The Seattle Times*

"Martel's honesty and deft writing avoid patronizing sentimentality. The [title] story proves he was a good writer long before *Life of Pi* ... Devotees of *Life of Pi* will be enchanted by *The Facts Behind the Helsinki Roccamatios*."
—*The Times-Picayune* (New Orleans)

"These unconventional stories are neither clumsy nor overstated. Even the two experimental pieces are surprisingly moving ... Like *Pi,* the stories pose questions about the nature of reality and effects of the past."
—*The Kansas City Star*

YANN MARTEL

The Facts Behind the Helsinki Roccamatios

A HARVEST BOOK
HARCOURT, INC.
Orlando   Austin   New York   San Diego   Toronto   London

www.HarcourtBooks.com

Library of Congress Cataloging-in-Publication Data
Martel, Yann.
The facts behind the Helsinki Roccamatios/Yann Martel.
p. cm.
I. Title.
PR9199.3.M3855F37   2004
813'.54—dc22   2004017505
ISBN-13: 978-0151-01090-5   ISBN-10: 0-15-101090-0
ISBN-13: 978-0156-03245-2 (pbk.)   ISBN-10: 0-15-603245-7 (pbk.)

Published in Canada in 2002 by Vintage Canada, a division of
Random House of Canada. First published in Canada by Alfred A. Knopf
Canada in 1993 and simultaneously in Great Britain by Faber and Faber.

The author would like to thank John Ralston Saul, Connie Rooke, and
Ellen Seligman for their help and encouragement.

Some of the facts behind the Helsinki Roccamatios are
based on information drawn from the following invaluable sources:
Canada's Illustrated Heritage (ed. Toivo Kiil); *The Canadian Encyclopedia*
(ed. James H. Marsh); *Encyclopedia Britannica*; and *An Encyclopedia
of World History* (ed. William L. Langer).

Three of these stories have previously appeared in slightly different form:
"The Facts Behind the Helsinki Roccamatios" and "The Time I Heard the
Private Donald J. Rankin String Concerto" in the *Malahat Review*, and
"Manners of Dying" in STORY.

Printed in the United States of America

First Harvest edition 2005

A C E G I K J H F D B

Contents

Author's Note

WHEN I WAS IN MY second year of university, aged nineteen, my studies ground to a halt. Just as the curtain was lifting on my adult life, with promises of untold freedom, what I might do with that freedom began to trouble me. I had always expected academic degrees—a bachelor's, a master's, a Ph.D.—to be the banister that would steady me up the steps of my successful life. But that year I stared at paragraphs of Immanuel Kant in a state of dumb incomprehension, I failed two courses and the banister fell away. The view gave me vertigo.

One consequence of this youthful existential crisis was my first creative effort, a one-act play I wrote over the course of three days. It was about a young man who falls in love with a door. When a friend finds out, he destroys the door. Our hero promptly commits suicide. It

was, without question, a terrible piece of writing, irre-
deemably blighted by immaturity. But I felt as though
I'd come upon a violin, picked it up and brought bow to
strings: the sound I made was perhaps terrible—but
what a beautiful instrument! There was something
deeply compelling about creating a setting, inventing
characters, giving them dialogue, directing them
through a plot, and by these means presenting my view
of life. For the first time, I had found an endeavour into
which I was willing to pour all my energies.

So I wrote. I wrote another play—an absurdist pas-
tiche, awful—before switching to prose. I wrote short
stories—all of them bad—before writing a novel—
equally bad—and then more short stories—none of
them good. To pursue the violin analogy, I drove the
neighbours crazy with my bad playing. But something
drew me on. It's not that I saw a future in it; to think
there was a link between my scribblings and books on
shelves was preposterous. I didn't think I was wasting
my time when I wrote—it was too exciting—but nor
did I think I was building a life. The fact is, I wasn't
thinking at all; I was just doing, madly, like Paganini
(without the talent).

Slowly, however, by dint of practice, I got better.
Here and there I struck a beautiful note. My developing sense was that the foundation of a story is an emotional foundation. If a story does not work emotionally,
it does not work at all. The emotion in question is not

the point; be it love, envy or apathy, so long as it is conveyed in a convincing manner, then the story will come alive. But a story must also stimulate the mind if it does not want to fade from memory. Intellect rooted in emotion, emotion structured by intellect—in other words, a *good idea* that *moves*—that was my lofty aim. When such an emotive idea came to me, when the spark of inspiration lit up my mind like a bonfire, the charge was like nothing I'd ever felt.

I got my inspiration anywhere and everywhere. Books. The newspaper. Movies. Music. Daily life. People I met. Memories and experience. And also from that mysterious creative ether whence ideas just popped into my head, unheralded. I put myself in a state of receptivity to stories. My eyes and ears sought them. I looked out, not in; in bored me. I did research with pleasure. Research was my way of learning, my own private university. Nothing delighted me more than to investigate the world for the sake of a story.

Meanwhile, I lived with my parents. Or, to be more accurate, I lived *off* my parents. I paid no rent, ate their food. I did short-term work—tree planting, dishwashing, working as a security guard—never letting these jobs get in the way of my pen. That I was doing nothing credible to ensure my future did not worry me (or my parents; thank God for them: all artists need patrons) because, to give just one example, I had a long story in mind—it might even be called a novella—

"Helsinki" for short. It was inspired by the death of a friend from AIDS. The title was unwieldy, the premise was awkward, the development was cumbersome. But there was life in it, the kind of life you find in a new-born child, in an exalted violin solo, the kind that makes everything fresh and hopeful and worth all the work. With that kind of life wriggling in my hands, how could I possibly worry about a bed and a pension for my senior years?

I sent stories out. Once I sent sixteen different stories to sixteen different literary reviews. I received sixteen rejections. Another time, it was nineteen stories to nineteen literary reviews. Two were accepted. That's a success rate of 5.7 percent. No matter. I would soldier on with my writing until something else came up. Nothing did, nothing has—and I'm happy for that.

The four stories in this collection are the best results of my early years as a writer. They did well. They won me some prizes. "Helsinki" was adapted to the stage and to the screen, "Manners of Dying" also to the screen and twice to the stage. First published as a book in Canada in 1993, the collection came out in six other countries. With these stories, the neighbours stopped banging on the walls and instead came over to say, "Bravo! Bravo!" It was a thrill for which I was—and still am—grateful.

Ten years on, I'm happy to offer these four stories

again to the reading public, slightly revised, the youthful urge to overstate reined in, the occasional clumsiness in the prose I hope ironed out. No doubt I have other stories to tell, but these four will always carry for me the joy and excitement of a world premiere.

The Facts
Behind
the
Helsinki
Roccamatios

pour J. G.

I HADN'T KNOWN PAUL for very long. We met in the fall of 1986 at Ellis University, in Roetown, just east of Toronto. I had taken time off and worked and travelled to India: I was twenty-three and in my last year. Paul had just turned nineteen and was entering first year. At the beginning of the year at Ellis, some senior students introduce the first-years to the university. There are no pranks or mischief or anything like that; the seniors are there to be helpful. They're called "amigos" and the first-years "amigees," which shows you how much Spanish they speak in Roetown. I was an amigo and most of my amigees struck me as cheerful, eager and young—very young. But right away I liked Paul's laidback, intelligent curiosity and his sceptical turn of mind. The two of us clicked and we started hanging out together. Because I was older and I had done more things, I usually spoke with the authority of a wise guru, and Paul listened like a young disciple—except when he raised an eyebrow and said something that threw my pompousness right into my face. Then we laughed and broke from these roles and it was plain what we were: really good friends.

Then, hardly into second term, Paul fell ill. Already at Christmas he had had a fever, and since then he had been carrying around a dry, hacking cough he couldn't get rid of. Initially, he—we—thought nothing of it. The cold, the dryness of the air—it was something to do with that.

Slowly things got worse. Now I recall signs that I didn't think twice about at the time. Meals left unfinished. A complaint once of diarrhea. A lack of energy that went beyond phlegmatic temperament. One day we were climbing the stairs to the library, hardly twenty-five steps, and when we reached the top, we stopped. I remember realizing that the only reason we had stopped was because Paul was out of breath and wanted to rest. And he seemed to be losing weight. It was hard to tell, what with the heavy winter sweaters and all, but I was certain that his frame had been stockier earlier in the year. When it became clear that something was wrong, we talked about it—nearly casually, you must understand—and I played doctor and said, "Let's see . . . breathlessness, cough, weight loss, fatigue. Paul, you have pneumonia." I was joking, of course; what do I know? But that's in fact what he had. It's called *Pneumocystis carinii* pneumonia, PCP to intimates. In mid-February Paul went to Toronto to see his family doctor.

Nine months later he was dead.

AIDS. He announced it to me over the phone in a detached voice. He had been gone nearly two weeks. He had just got back from the hospital, he told me. I reeled. My first thoughts were for myself. Had he ever cut himself in my presence? If so, what had happened? Had I ever drunk from his glass? Shared his food? I tried to establish if there had ever been a bridge between his system and mine. Then I thought of him. I thought of gay sex and hard drugs. But Paul wasn't gay. He had never told me so outright, but I knew him well enough and I had never detected the least ambivalence. I likewise couldn't imagine him a heroin addict. In any case, that wasn't it. Three years ago, when he was sixteen, he had gone to Jamaica on a Christmas holiday with his parents. They had had a car accident. Paul's right leg had been broken and he'd lost some blood. He had received a blood transfusion at the local hospital. Six witnesses of the accident had come along to volunteer blood. Three were of the right blood group. Several phone calls and a little research turned up the fact that one of the three had died unexpectedly two years later while being treated for pneumonia. An autopsy had revealed that the man had severe toxoplasmic cerebral lesions. A suspicious combination.

I went to visit Paul that weekend at his home in wealthy Rosedale. I didn't want to; I wanted to block the whole thing off mentally. I asked—this was my excuse—if he was sure his parents cared for a visitor. He insisted that I come. And I did. I came through. I drove down to Toronto. And I was right about his parents. Because what hurt most that first weekend was not Paul, but Paul's family.

After learning how he had probably caught the virus, Paul's father, Jack, didn't utter a syllable for the rest of that day. Early the next morning he fetched the tool kit in the basement, put his winter parka over his housecoat, stepped out onto the driveway, and proceeded to destroy the family car. Because he had been the driver when they had had the accident in Jamaica, even though it hadn't been his fault and it had been in another car, a rental. He took a hammer and shattered all the lights and windows. He scraped and trashed the entire body. He banged nails into the tires. He siphoned the gasoline from the tank, poured it over and inside the car, and set it on fire. That's when neighbours called the firefighters. They rushed to the scene and put the fire out. The police came, too. When he blurted out why he had done it, all of them were very understanding and the police left without charging him or anything; they only asked if he wanted to go to the hospital, which he didn't. So that was the first thing I saw when I walked up to Paul's large, corner-lot house:

a burnt wreck of a Mercedes covered in dried foam.

Jack was a hard-working corporate lawyer. When Paul introduced me to him, he grinned, shook my hand hard and said, "Good to meet you!" Then he didn't seem to have anything else to say. His face was red. Paul's mother, Mary, was in their bedroom. I had met her at the beginning of the university year. As a young woman she had earned an M.A. in anthropology from McGill, she had been a highly ranked amateur tennis player, and she had travelled. Now she worked part-time for a human rights organization. Paul was proud of his mother and got along with her very well. She was a smart, energetic woman. But here she was, lying awake on the bed in a fetal position, looking like a wrinkled balloon, all the taut vitality drained out of her. Paul stood next to the bed and just said, "My mother." She barely reacted. I didn't know what to do. Paul's sister, Jennifer, a graduate student in sociology at the University of Toronto, was the most visibly distraught. Her eyes were red, her face was puffy—she looked terrible. I don't mean to be funny, but even George H., the family Labrador, was grief-stricken. He had squeezed himself under the living-room sofa, wouldn't budge, and whined all the time.

The verdict had come on Wednesday morning, and since then (it was Friday) none of them, George H. included, had eaten a morsel of food. Paul's father and mother hadn't gone to work, and Jennifer hadn't gone to school. They slept, when they slept, wherever they happened to be. One morning I found Paul's father sleeping on the living-room floor, fully dressed and wrapped in the Persian rug, a hand reaching for the dog beneath the sofa. Except for frenzied bursts of phone conversation, the house was quiet.

In the middle of it all was Paul, who wasn't reacting. At a funeral where the family members are broken with pain and grief, he was the funeral director going about with professional calm and dull sympathy. Only on the third day of my stay did he start to react. But death couldn't make itself understood. Paul knew that something awful was happening to him, but he couldn't grasp it. Death was beyond him. It was a theoretical abstraction. He spoke of his condition as if it were news from a foreign country. He said, "I'm going to die," the way he might say, "There was a ferry disaster in Bangladesh."

I had meant to stay just the weekend—there was school—but I ended up staying ten days. I did a lot of housecleaning and cooking during that time. The family didn't notice much, but that was all right. Paul helped me, and he liked that because it gave him something to do. We had the car towed away, we replaced a phone that Paul's father had destroyed, we cleaned the house spotlessly from top to bottom, we gave George H. a bath (George H. because Paul really liked the Beatles and when he was a kid he liked to say to himself when he was walking the dog, "At this very moment, unbeknown to anyone, absolutely incognito, Beatle Paul and Beatle George are walking the streets of Toronto," and he would dream about what it would be like to sing "Help!" in Shea Stadium or something like that), and we went food shopping and nudged the family into eating. I say "we" and "Paul helped"—what I mean is that I did everything while he sat in a chair nearby. Drugs called dapsone and trimethoprim were overcoming Paul's pneumonia, but he was still weak and out of breath. He moved about like an old man, slowly and conscious of every exertion.

It took the family a while to break out of its shock. During the course of Paul's illness I noticed three states they would go through. In the first, common at home, when the pain was too close, they would pull away and each do their thing: Paul's father would destroy something sturdy, like a table or an appliance, Paul's mother would lie on her bed in a daze, Jennifer would cry in her bedroom, and George H. would hide under the sofa and whine. In the second, at the hospital often, they would rally around Paul, and they would talk and sob and encourage each other and laugh and whisper. Finally, in the third, they would display what I suppose you could call normal behaviour, an ability to get through the day as if death didn't exist, a composed, somewhat numb face of courage that, because it was required every single day, became both heroic and ordinary. The family went through these states over the course of several months, or in an hour.

I DON'T WANT TO talk about what AIDS does to a body. Imagine it very bad—and then make it worse (you can't imagine the degradation). Look up in the dictionary the word "flesh"—such a plump word—and then look up the word "melt."

That's not the worst of it, anyway. The worst of it is the resistance put up, the I'm-not-going-to-die virus. It's the one that affects the most people because it attacks the living, the ones who surround and love the dying. That virus infected me early on. I remember the day precisely. Paul was in the hospital. He was eating his supper, his whole supper, till the plate was clean and shiny, though he wasn't at all hungry. I watched him as he chased down every last pea with his fork and as he consciously chewed every mouthful before swallowing. *It will help my body fight. Every little bit counts*—that's what he was thinking. It was written all over his face, all over his body, all over the walls. I wanted to scream, "Forget the fucking peas, Paul. You're going to die! DIE!" Except that the words "death" and "dying," and their various derivatives and synonyms, were now tacitly forbidden from our talk. So I just sat there, my face emptied of any expression, anger roiling me up inside. My condition got much worse every time I saw Paul shave. All he had were a few downy whiskers on his chin; he just wasn't the hairy type. Still, he began to shave every day. Every day he lathered up his face with a mountain of shaving cream and scraped it off with a disposable razor. It's an image that has become engraved in my memory: a vacillatingly healthy Paul dressed in a hospital gown standing in front of a mirror, turning his head this way and that, pulling his skin here and there, meticulously doing something that was utterly, utterly useless.

I botched my academic year. I was skipping lectures and seminars constantly and I couldn't write any essays. In fact, I couldn't even read anymore; I would stare for hours at the same paragraph of Kant or Heidegger, trying to understand what it was saying, trying to focus, without any success. At the same time, I developed a loathing for my country. Canada reeked of insipidity, comfort and insularity. Canadians were up to their necks in materialism and above the neck it was all American television. Nowhere could I see idealism or rigour. There was nothing but deadening mediocrity. Canada's policy on Central America, on Native issues, on the environment, on Reagan's America, on everything, made my stomach turn. There was nothing about this country that I liked, nothing. I couldn't wait to escape.

One day in a philosophy seminar—that was my major—I was doing a presentation on Hegel's philosophy of history. The professor, an intelligent and considerate man, interrupted me and asked me to elucidate a point he hadn't understood. I fell silent. I looked about the cosy, book-filled office where we were sitting. I remember that moment of silence very clearly because it was precisely then, rising through my confusion with unstoppable force, that I boiled over with anger and cynicism. I screamed, I got up, I projected the hefty Hegel book through the closed window, and I stormed out of the office, slamming the door as hard as I could and kicking in one of its nicely sculptured panels for good measure.

I tried to withdraw from Ellis, but I missed the deadline. I appealed and appeared in front of a committee, the Committee on Undergraduate Standings and Petitions, CUSP they call it. My grounds for withdrawing were Paul, but when the chairman of CUSP prodded me and asked me in a glib little voice what exactly I meant by "emotional distress," I looked at him and I decided that Paul's agony wasn't an orange I was going to peel and quarter and present to him. This time, however, I didn't make a scene. I just said, "I've changed my mind. I would like to withdraw my petition. Thank you for your attention," and I walked out.

As a result I failed my year. I didn't care and I don't care. I hung around Roetown, a nice place to hang around.

————

BUT WHAT I REALLY WANT to tell you about, the purpose of this story, is the Roccamatio family of Helsinki. That's not Paul's family; his last name was Atsee. Nor is it my family.

You see, Paul spent months in the hospital. When his condition was stable he came home, but mostly I remember him at the hospital. The course of his illnesses, tests and treatments became the course of his life. Against my will I became familiar with words like azidothymidine, alpha interferon, domipramine, nitrazepam. (When you're with people who are really sick, you discover what an illusion science can be.) I visited Paul. I was making the trip to Toronto to see him once or twice during the week, and often on weekends too, and I was calling him every day. When I was there, if he was strong enough, we would go for a walk or see a movie or a play. Mostly, though, we just sat around. But when you're between four walls and neither of you wants to watch television anymore, and the papers have been read, and you're sick of playing cards, chess, Scrabble and Trivial Pursuit, and you can't always be talking about *it* and *its* progress, you run out of ways to whittle away the time. Which was fine. Neither Paul nor I minded just sitting there, listening to music, lost in our own thoughts.

Except that I started feeling we should do something with that time. I don't mean put on togas and ruminate philosophically about life, death, God, the universe and the meaning of it all. We had done that in first term, before we even knew he was sick. That's the staple of undergraduate life, isn't it? What else is there to talk about when you've stayed up all night till sunrise? Or when you've just read Descartes or Berkeley or T.S. Eliot for the first time? And anyway, Paul was nineteen. What are you at nineteen? You're a blank page. You're all hopes and dreams and uncertainties. You're all future and little philosophy. What I meant was that between the two of us we had to do something constructive, something that would make something out of nothing, sense out of nonsense, something that would go beyond *talking* about life, death, God, the universe and the meaning of it all and actually *be* those things.

I gave it a good thinking. I had plenty of time to think: in the spring I got a job as a gardener for the city of Roetown. I spent my days tending flowerbeds, clipping shrubbery and mowing lawns, work that kept my hands busy but left my mind free.

The idea came to me one day as I was pushing a gas mower across an expanse of municipal lawn, my ears muffled by industrial ear protectors. Two words stopped me dead in my tracks: Boccaccio's *Decameron*. I had read a beaten-up copy of the Italian classic when I was in India. Such a simple idea: an isolated villa outside of Florence; the world dying of the Black Death; ten people gathered together hoping to survive; *telling each other stories to pass the time.*

That was it. The transformative wizardry of the imagination. Boccaccio had done it in the fourteenth century, we would do it in the twentieth: we would tell each other stories. But we would be the sick this time, not the world, and we wouldn't be fleeing it, either. On the contrary: with our stories we would be remembering the world, re-creating it, embracing it. Yes, to meet as storytellers to embrace the world—there, that was how Paul and I would destroy the void.

The more I thought about it, the more I liked it. Paul and I would create a story about a family, a large family, to allow diverse yet related stories, to ensure continuity and development. The family would be Canadian and the setting would be contemporary, to make the historical and cultural references easy. I would have to be a firm guide and not let the stories slide into mere autobiography. And I would have to be well prepared so that I could carry the story all by myself when Paul was too weak or depressed. I would also have to convince him that he had no choice, that this storytelling wasn't a game or something on the same level as watching a movie or talking about politics. He would have to see that everything besides the story was useless, even his desperate existential thoughts that did nothing but frighten him. Only the imaginary must count.

But the imaginary doesn't spring from nothing. If our story was to have any stamina, any breadth and

depth, if it was to avoid both literal reality and irrele-
vant fantasy, it would need a structure, a guideline of
sorts, some curb along which we blind could tap our
white canes. I racked my brains trying to find just such
a structure. We needed something firm yet loose, that
would both restrict us and inspire us.

I hit upon it while picking weeds: we would use the
history of the twentieth century. Not that the story
would start in 1901 and progress up to 1986—that
wouldn't be much of a blueprint. Rather, the twentieth
century would be our mould; we would use one event
from each year as a metaphorical guideline. It would be
a story in eighty-six episodes, each episode echoing one
event from one year of the unfolding century.

To have figured out what to make of my time with
Paul electrified me. I was bursting with ideas. Nothing
struck me as more worthwhile than making the trip
from Roetown to Toronto—commuting, imagine; that
dull, work-related chore—to invent stories with Paul.

I explained it to him carefully. It was at the hospital. He was undergoing tests.

"I don't get it," he said. "What do you mean by
'metaphorical guideline'? And when does the story take
place?"

"Nowadays. The family exists right now. The historical events we choose will be a parallel, something to
guide us in making up our stories about the family. Like

Homer's *Odyssey* was a parallel for Joyce when he was writing *Ulysses.*"

"I've never read *Ulysses.*"

"That doesn't matter. The point is, the novel takes place in Dublin on a single day in 1904, but it's named after an ancient Greek epic. Joyce used the ten years' wandering of Ulysses after the Trojan War as a parallel for his story in Dublin. His story is a metaphorical transformation of *The Odyssey.*"

"Why don't we just read the book aloud since I've never read it?"

"Because we don't want to be spectators, Paul."

"Oh."

"To start with, we have to decide where the family lives."

He was looking at me blankly. He was sceptical— and tired. I insisted. I even got a touch annoyed. I didn't use any of the D words, but they were in the air. His face crumpled and he started to cry. I apologized immediately. Yes, we would read *Ulysses* aloud, what a good idea. And then—why not?—*War and Peace.*

I had left his room, was stepping into the elevator, when a long shout exploded in the corridor.

"Helsinkiiiiiiiiiiiiiiiiiiiiiiiii!"

I smiled. You see, Paul and I were on the same wavelength. We were young, and the young can be radical. We're not encrusted with habits and traditions. If we catch ourselves in time, we can start all over. So the story would take place in Helsinki, the capital of Finland. A good choice. A faraway city where neither of us had been would be much easier for our fancy to play with than one that was right in front of our eyes. I returned to Paul's room. His face was still red from shouting.

I asked him about the name of the family. He pouted his lips and narrowed his eyes and thought for a moment. Then he expelled a sound: "Roccamatio." *What?* "The Roccamatios—Rok-kah-MAH-tee-ohs." I wasn't keen on that one. Not very realistic. Something more Nordic-sounding might be better, no? But Paul insisted: the Roccamatios—Rok-kah-MAH-tee-ohs, he repeated—were a Finnish family of Italian extraction. So be it. The Helsinki Roccamatios were located and baptized. Their story was waiting to be told. We agreed on the rules: I would be the judge of what was fictionally acceptable; transparent autobiography was forbidden. The story would take place nowadays, the mid-1980s. Each episode would be related in one sitting and would resemble one event from a consecutive year of the twentieth century. We would alternate in telling the story; I would have the odd years, Paul would have the even years. We discussed what we knew about Helsinki and agreed on the following: one, it had a population of a million inhabitants; two, it was the capital of Finland in every way—political, commercial, industrial, cultural, etc.; three, it was an important port; four, it had a small but fractious Swedish-speaking minority; and five, Russia always weighed heavily on the mood of the nation. Finally, we agreed that the Roccamatios would be a secret between the two of us.

We decided that after a period of reflection and research, I would start with the first episode. I brought Paul a pen, some paper, and a three-volume work called *A History of the 20th Century.* His father set a small bookcase with wheels beside his bed and filled it with all thirty-two volumes of the 15th edition of *Encyclopaedia Britannica.*

Now understand that you're not going to hear the story of the Helsinki Roccamatios. Certain intimacies shouldn't be made public. They should be known to exist, that's all. The telling of the story of the Roccamatios was difficult, especially as the years went by. We started brave and strong, arguing all the time and interrupting each other constantly, surprising ourselves with our cleverness and originality, laughing a whole lot—but it's so tiring to re-create the world when you're not at the peak of health. Paul wouldn't be so much unwilling—he would still object or redirect me with a word or a scowl—as unable. Even listening became tiring.

The story of the Helsinki Roccamatios was often whispered. And it wasn't whispered to you. Of these AIDS years, all I have kept—outside my head—is this record:

The Facts Behind the Helsinki Roccamatios

1901—After a reign of sixty-four years, Queen Victoria dies. Her reign has witnessed a period of incredible industrial expansion and increasing material prosperity. In its own blinkered and delusional way, the Victorian age has been the happiest of all—an age of stability, order, wealth, enlightenment and hope. Science and technology are new and triumphant, and Utopia seems at hand.

I begin with an ending, with the death of Sandro Roccamatio, the patriarch of the family. It is dramatic, and it allows me to introduce the family members, who are all at the funeral.

1902—Under the forceful leadership of Clifford Sifton, Prime Minister Wilfrid Laurier's Minister of the Interior, the settlement of Canada's west is in full swing. Sifton sends out millions of pamphlets in dozens of languages and strings a net of agents across northern and central Europe. Ships that have just dumped their Canadian wheat on the Old Continent bring home the catch. In less than a decade the population of the Prairies increases by a million inhabitants and wheat production jumps fivefold. Laurier proclaims to the booming country, "The twentieth century belongs to Canada."

1903— Orville and Wilbur Wright fly at Kill Devil Hills, North Carolina. Their powered machine, Flyer I *(now popularly called* Kitty Hawk*), stays in the air for twelve seconds on its first flight, fifty-nine seconds on its fourth and last.*

1904— As a direct result of the Dreyfus affair, Prime Minister Emile Combes of France introduces a bill for the complete separation of Church and State. The bill guarantees complete liberty of conscience, removes the State from having any say in the appointment of ecclesiastics or in the payment of their salaries, and severs all other connections between Church and State.

A routine to our storytelling has already developed. It's nearly a ceremony. First, and always first, we shake hands every time we meet, like the Europeans. Paul takes pleasure in this, I can tell. If there's a need, we deal with health and therapy. Then we small-talk, usually about politics since we're both diligent newspaper readers. Finally, after a short pause to collect ourselves, we get on with the Roccamatios.

1905— The German monthly Annalen der Physik *publishes papers by Albert Einstein, a twenty-six-year-old German Jew who works as an examiner in a patent office* *in Bern, Switzerland. The Special Theory of Relativity is born. There is energy everywhere. $E = mc^2$, as Einstein puts it.*

1906—Tommy Burns defeats Marvin Hart to become the first (and only) Canadian to win the world heavyweight boxing championship. Burns defends his title eleven times in three years, notably knocking out the Irish champion Jem Roche in 1 minute and 28 seconds, the shortest heavy-weight title defence ever.

Paul is nearly well. He is plagued by minor ills—night sweating here, diarrhea there—and a lack of energy, but it's nothing unmanageable. He is at home, and as he has never been sick a day in his life until now, the routine of illness has an exotic appeal. He is started on a pro-gram of azidothymidine (AZT) and multivitamins, and he visits the hospital every week, sometimes stay-ing overnight. He likes the hospital. The omnipotent men and women in white, their scientific jargon, the innumerable tests, the impeccable cleanliness of the place—they exhaust and reassure him. His mood is good.

We make plans. We speak of travel. I have travelled some, Paul less, mostly with his family, and we both see travel as essential to growth, as a state of being, as a metaphor for inner journeying. Disdaining the well-worn path, we hardly speak of Europe. We are magi, not tourists. After touching on Iceland, Portugal, Bulgaria and Poland, our star leads us to other lands, to Turkey and Yemen, to Mexico and Peru and Bolivia, to South Africa and the Philippines, to India and Nepal.

1907—A new strain of wheat, Marquis, is sent out to Indian Head, Saskatchewan, for testing. It is the result of an exhaustive scientific selection process, the credit for which goes to Charles Edwards Saunders, cerealist at the Ottawa Experimental Farm. The new strain's response to Saskatchewan conditions is phenomenal. It is resistant to heavy winds and to disease, and it produces high yields that make excellent flour. Most importantly it matures early, thus avoiding the damage of frost and greatly extending the areas of Alberta and Saskatchewan where wheat can be grown. By 1920, Marquis will make up 90 percent of prairie spring wheat, helping make Canada one of the great bread-baskets of the world.

If I'm not distracted by my job or by thoughts of food, transportation and the like, I think of the Roccamatios. They are my mind's natural focus. I have to find historical events. Then I have to think of plot and parallel, of the way in which my story will resemble the historical event, whether in an obvious way or a subtle way, for one symbolic moment (at the beginning or at the end?) or all along. These thoughts pester me, challenge me, make me go on. I am hardly aware of my workaday life.

1908—Ernest Thompson Seton, author, naturalist and artist, organizes the Boy Scouts of Canada. The aim of the organization, like that of the Girl Guides founded two years later, is to foster good citizenship, decent behaviour, love of nature, and skill in various outdoor activities. The Scouts follow a moral code and are encouraged to perform a daily good deed. They go camping, swimming, sailing and hiking. They undertake community service projects. Their motto is "Be Prepared," and they shake hands with the left hand.

I had not envisioned the Roccamatios so ambitiously. Marriages, the runaway daughter, the bitter but liberating divorce, childbirth, entrepreneurial success, romance, community leadership—they are a dynamic family. Paul and I go about them briskly. I meant for us to alternate years, but so far they have been more of a co-operative invention.

But there are clouds on the horizon. The year 1909 is mine. I see trial and error in the story I make of it. Paul sees trial and fraud. It's the first time we quibble. And I'm troubled by his story for 1910.

1909—Commander Robert E. Peary, on his third attempt, claims to reach the North Pole. Though generally accepted, the claim is questioned by many because of the inadequacy of his observations and the incredible timetable of travelling he has submitted.

1910—Japan, increasingly militaristic and determined to expand its power and influence, annexes Korea and begins to exploit the country's people and resources entirely for its own benefit. Koreans are denied freedom of speech, of assembly and association, even of going to school in their own language.

I launch the Roccamatios into the hurly-burly of Helsinki municipal politics!

1911—A federal election is called in Canada. The dominant issue of the campaign is reciprocity, an agreement to lower tariffs between Canada and the United States. Liberal Prime Minister Wilfrid Laurier favours reciprocity. Conservative Opposition leader Robert Borden does not. Eastern Canadian manufacturers cry that such an economic accord will be the first step in a political takeover. Certain statements by influential Americans—"I hope to see the day when the American flag will float over every square foot of the British North American possessions,

clear to the North Pole," says Champ Clark, Speaker of the
House of Representatives—seem to justify those fears.
Laurier and his Liberals go down to a resounding defeat,
and Borden becomes prime minister.

Paul's moods are changing. I think he's starting to realize what he's in for. Initially his pills and injections were a source of delight. *Here comes health*, they signalled to him. *You'll beat this.* But health eludes him, and he's angry about it. He still takes his medicines religiously, but they taste bitter now, not sweet. In 1912, the Minimum Wage law is passed in England; Roald Amundsen reaches the South Pole; a beautiful bust of Queen Nefertiti is discovered in Egypt by German archaeologists; Edgar Rice Burroughs publishes his first Tarzan stories; Marcel Duchamp shows his *Nude Descending a Staircase, No. 2.* But Paul will have none of these. His story, about a mugging, is plain, simple and brutal.

1912—After a siege of five hours in Choisy-le-Roy, a suburb of Paris, anarchist Jules Joseph Bonnot is killed. Bonnot and his gang, la bande à Bonnot as they are known, have been terrorizing French society with the jaunty unconcern with which they shoot tellers, guards, passers-by, policemen, dwellers and drivers during their bare-faced bank robberies, break-ins and car thefts. In the final attack on his holdout,

*the authorities deploy against a solitary Bonnot three ar-
tillery regiments and five police brigades, and they use guns,
heavy machine guns and dynamite. Bonnot is found, still
alive, wrapped in a mattress. He is finished off. There are
more than thirty thousand spectators at the siege.*

Lasting optimism has one essential ally: reason. Any
optimism that is unreasonable is bound to be dashed by
reality, leading to even more unhappiness. Optimism,
therefore, must always be illuminated by the gentle,
purging light of reason and be unshakeably grounded in
sanity of mind, so that pessimism becomes a foolish,
short-sighted attitude. What this means—reasonable-
ness being the tepid, inglorious thing it is—is that optimism can arise only from small but undeniable
achievements. In 1913, I put my best foot forward.

1913—The zipper is patented.

Paul has been hospitalized. He's having a relapse of
Pneumocystis carinii. He's put on dapsone and trimethoprim again, but this time he suffers side effects: a fever,
and a rash all over his neck and chest. He's amazingly
thin; he hardly eats and his diarrhea is intractable. He
has a tube up his nose. In his story, Marco Roccamatio

has a serious fall-out with his brother Orlando.

1914—*In Sarajevo, for the sake of a South Slav nationalist dream, nineteen-year-old Gavrilo Princip pulls the trig-
ger of his revolver and starts the First World War.*

> *Austria declares war on Serbia.*
>
> *Germany declares war on Russia.*
>
> *Germany declares war on France.*
>
> *Germany declares war on Belgium.*
>
> *Great Britain (and with her Canada, India,
> Australia, New Zealand, South Africa and
> Newfoundland) declares war on Germany.*
>
> *Montenegro declares war on Austria.*
>
> *Austria declares war on Russia.*
>
> *Serbia declares war on Germany.*
>
> *Montenegro declares war on Germany.*
>
> *France declares war on Austria.*
>
> *Great Britain declares war on Austria.*
>
> *Japan declares war on Germany.*
>
> *Japan declares war on Austria.*
>
> *Austria declares war on Belgium.*
>
> *Russia declares war on Turkey.*
>
> *Serbia declares war on Turkey.*
>
> *Great Britain declares war on Turkey.*
>
> *France declares war on Turkey.*
>
> *Egypt declares war on Turkey.*

I tell Paul 1914 was the year the Panama Canal was opened and wouldn't it make for a more pleasant story?

"Your history is biased," he replies.

"So is yours," I shoot back.

"But mine is the correct bias."

"How do you know?"

"Because it accounts for the future."

I can't understand it. I have read of people who have AIDS who live for years. Yet week by week Paul is getting thinner and weaker. He is receiving treatments, yes, but they don't seem to be doing much, except for his pneumonia. Anyway, he doesn't seem to have any particular illness, just a wasting away. I ask a doctor about it, nearly complain about it. He's standing in a doorway. He listens to my litany silently—he's a big, unshaven man and his eyes are red—and then he doesn't say anything and finally he says in a low, measured voice, "We're—doing—our—best."

It's my turn. I must be careful. I refuse to invoke the war. I would like the extension of suffrage to women in Denmark. But a story of reconciliation would not please Paul. I consider the publication of Kafka's *Metamorphosis*. It's too dark. I must neither give in to Paul, nor ignore him. I must steer between total abstraction and grim reality. I don't know what to do. I go for the ambiguous.

1915—Alfred Wegener, a German meteorologist and geo-physicist, publishes The Origin of Continents and Oceans, *in which he gives the classic expression of the controversial theory of continental drift. Wegener postu-lates that a mother landmass, which he names Pangaea, broke up some 250 million years ago, the pieces drifting apart at the rate of roughly an inch a year, thus producing the continents of today.*

"An inch a year?" Paul smiles. He likes my story, too. But he won't be stopped.

1916— Germany declares war on Portugal.
Austria declares war on Portugal.
Romania declares war on Austria.
Italy declares war on Germany.
Germany declares war on Romania.
Turkey declares war on Romania.
Bulgaria declares war on Romania.

More tests. Paul has something called *cytomegalovirus,* which may account for his diarrhea and his general weakness. It's a highly disseminating infection, could affect his eyes, lungs, liver, gastrointestinal tract, spinal cord or brain. There's nothing to be done. No effective therapy exists. Paul is speechlessly depressed. I give in to him.

>1917—*The United States declares war on Germany.*
>*Panama declares war on Germany.*
>*Cuba declares war on Germany.*
>*Greece declares war on Austria, Bulgaria, Germany and Turkey.*
>*Siam declares war on Germany and Austria.*
>*Liberia declares war on Germany.*
>*China declares war on Germany and Austria.*
>*Brazil declares war on Germany.*
>*The United States declares war on Austria.*
>*Panama declares war on Austria.*
>*Cuba declares war on Austria.*

For 1918 Paul wants to use further declarations of war—Haiti and Honduras declared war on Germany, he informs me—but for the first time I use my power of veto and declare these fictionally unacceptable. Nor do I accept the publication of Oswald Spengler's *The Decline of the West*, in which Spengler argues that civilizations are like natural organisms, with life cycles implying birth, bloom and decay, and that Western civilization has entered the last, inevitable stage of decay. Enough is enough, I tell Paul. There is hope. The sun still shines. Paul is angry, but he is tired and he submits. I think he was expecting my censure, for he surprises me with a curious event and a fully prepared story.

> *1918—After an extensive study of globular clusters—immense, densely packed groups of stars—Harlow Shapley determines that the centre of the Milky Way Galaxy, our galaxy, is in the Sagittarius constellation and that our solar system lies about two thirds of the way from this centre, some thirty thousand light years away.*

"Isn't it grand," I say.

"Aren't we lonely," he replies.

His story—of Orlando, of alcoholism—is ugly.

> *1919—Walter Gropius becomes head of the Bauhaus, a school of art, design and architecture in Weimar, Germany. Under his leadership, the teachers at Bauhaus break with the past. They emphasize geometrical forms, smooth surfaces, regular outlines, primary colours and modern materials. Just as importantly, they take to mass-manufacturing techniques, making their functional, aesthetically pleasing objects affordable to everyone. Never before have objects of daily life looked so good to so many.*

"This AZT is exhausting," says Paul. He is anemic because of it and receives blood transfusions regularly.

In 1920, I forbid the publication of Freud's *Beyond the Pleasure Principle,* in which Freud posits an underlying, destructive drive, Thanatos, the death instinct, which seeks to end life's inevitable tensions by ending life itself. Paul changes historical events while keeping the same Roccamatio story.

1920—Dada triumphs. Born in Zurich during the depths of the First World War and spread by a merry, desperate band of writers and artists, including Hugo Ball, Tristan Tzara, Marcel Duchamp, Jean Arp, Richard Hulsenbeck, Raoul Hausmann, Kurt Schwitters, Francis Picabia, George Grosz and many others, Dadaism seeks the demolition of all the values of art, society and civilization.

Paul tells me over the phone that he's developing Kaposi's sarcoma. He has purple, blue lesions on his feet and ankles. Not many, but they are there. The doctors have zeroed in on them. He will be put on alpha interferon and undergo radiation therapy. Paul's voice is shaky. But we agree, we strongly agree, with what the doctors have said, that radiation therapy has been found to be successful against localized Kaposi's sarcoma, and he's only got it on his skin, in fact, only on his feet, and it doesn't hurt, and at least his lungs are fine. I promise to come by the hospital.

Paul is quiet. He is in his usual, favourite position: lying on his back against a fastidiously constructed pyramid of three pillows.

1921—Frederick Banting and Charles Best discover insulin, the glucose-metabolizing hormone secreted by the pancreas. It is immediately and spectacularly effective as a therapy for diabetes. The lives of millions are saved.

I have just started my story when Paul interrupts me.

"In 1921, Albert Camus died in a car crash."

He doesn't say anything more. I continue until he interrupts me a second time.

"In 1921, Albert Camus died in a car crash."

"Paul, he didn't. Camus died in 1960."

"No, Albert Camus died in a car crash in 1921. He was a passenger in a Facel-Vega. Never heard of it, have you? It was a small series, French copy of a Chrysler, not very road-tested. Camus and some friends were returning—"

"Paul, what are you doing?"

"They were returning to Paris from the Lubéron, where Camus had bought a beautiful white house with his Nobel money. The road was—"

"Okay, that's enough."

"The road was straight and dry and empty. Along the road were trees. Suddenly—an axle that broke? a wheel that blocked?—for no reason, the car—"

"You're not following the rules, Paul. You're chea—"

"THE CAR SLID and hit a tree. Camus was killed instantly—"

"In 1921, Banting and Best isolate insulin, the glu—"

"In 1921, Camus was killed instantly—"

"The glucose-metabolizing hormone—"

"By a tree—"

"By a hormone—"

"In 1921, the atomic bomb was dropped on Hiroshima and it killed—"

"Ha! In 1921, Banting and Best—"

"In 1921, the bomb was dropped and it killed—"

"It is spectacularly effective as—"

"It killed—"

"Is spectacularly effective—"

"It ki—"

"Is effective."

"It—"

"So, *so* effective."

He's tiring; I can sense he will submit in a moment. "IT WAS DROPPED AND IT KILLED CAMUS!"

He shrieks this in a tone of voice that chills me and

shuts me up instantly. He's glaring at me, wild-eyed. I'm thinking, *What have you done, you idiot?* when he lunges for me. I'm startled and pull back, but he's going to fall to the floor, so I catch him. I'm amazed at how light he feels. He punches me twice in the face, but he's so weak it doesn't hurt. He begins to sob.

"It's all right, Paul, it's all right. I'm sorry," I tell him softly. "It's all right. I'm sorry. Take it easy. Listen, I've got something better. In 1921, they didn't discover insulin. In 1921, Sacco and Vanzetti were sentenced to death. Sacco and Vanzetti, Paul, Sacco and Vanzetti, Sacco and Vanzetti."

His tears are flooding his face and dripping onto my arms. I lift him and push him back onto the bed.

"Sacco and Vanzetti, Paul, Sacco and Vanzetti. It's all right. I'm sorry. Sacco and Vanzetti, Sacco and Vanzetti, Sacco and Vanzetti."

I get a wet facecloth and wipe my arms and gently wipe his face. I comb his hair with my fingers.

"It's all right, Paul. Sacco and Vanzetti, Sacco and Vanzetti, Sacco and Vanzetti, Sacco and Vanzetti."

I improvise a grim story. Sometimes our stories are short on plot, but by means of details left unexplained, by means of fertile ambiguities, they nonetheless resonate in the way of a painting, static but rich. But here it's not at all like that. There is little plot and little meaning. The story just stumbles along, unbelievable, unexplainable. Loretta Roccamatio drowns herself.

*1921—Nicola Sacco and Bartolomeo Vanzetti, both poor
Italian immigrants and anarchists, are found guilty and
sentenced to death for two murders committed during a
robbery in South Braintree, Massachusetts. In spite of
flaws in the evidence, irregularities at their trial, accusations that the judge and jury were prejudiced against their
political beliefs and social status, evidence that pointed to a
known criminal gang, in spite of worldwide protests and appeals for clemency, Sacco and Vanzetti will be executed in
1927.*

Paul is put on anti-depressants—amitriptyline at first,
then domipramine. It will take about two weeks before
they become effective. In the meantime he is kept
under close surveillance, especially at night, when he
sleeps only in fits. The clinical psychologist comes by
nearly every afternoon. I call Paul up to six times a day.

*1922—Benito Mussolini, at the age of thirty-nine, becomes
the youngest prime minister in Italian history, and the first
of Europe's 20th-century fascist dictators.*

"I can feel them in my blood. I can feel each virus as it
flows up my arm, crosses my chest, goes into my heart,
and then shoots out to one of my legs. And I can't do

anything. I just lie here waiting, knowing it's going to get worse," he says.

He's so fragile. I give in to him again.

1923—Germany is incapable of making its payments on the war reparations imposed by the Allies in the Treaty of Versailles (set at the equivalent of thirty-three billion dollars). France and Belgium occupy the Ruhr district to force compliance. The German government blocks all reparation deliveries and encourages passive resistance. The French and Belgians respond with mass arrests and an economic blockade. The German economy is devastated, and its government begins to founder. The ground is fertile for extremists.

Paul is plainly waiting for me. He's bored. Strange how this illness, which aims to rob him of time, leaves him with so much of it on his hands.

1924—Vladimir Lenin, whose health has been precarious for the last eighteen months, dies of a stroke at the age of fifty-four. The secretary general of the Communist Party's Central Committee, Joseph Stalin, whom Lenin had unsuccessfully tried to remove, starts an extravagant cult of the deceased leader, thus portraying himself as Lenin's greatest defender.

I bump into Paul's parents as I'm leaving the hospital. I have gotten to know them well. They have taken to me, as I have to them. I used to call ahead when I was visiting Paul at home, but quickly I was given a key and told that I was welcome any hour of the day or night, seven days a week, no knock on the door required. It's as though I have three parents now instead of one (my father died when I was ten): Jack pats me on the back, and Mary smiles and rests her fingers lightly on my forearm as she tells me that there are mocha yogurts in the fridge, my favourite.

1925—Adolf Hitler publishes The Settlement of Accounts, *the first volume of his political manifesto,* Mein Kampf (My Struggle). *"All who are not of good race are chaff," he writes. Germans "must occupy themselves not merely with the breeding of dogs, horses and cats but also with the purity of their own blood." The book is pompous in style, repetitious, meandering, illogical, and filled with grammatical mistakes. The ranting of a half-educated nut.*

I should have gone for a better story; Paul seems to be improving. His Kaposi is uncertain, but his diarrhea is nearly gone.

*1926—Rudolf Valentino, through the intercession of a rup-
tured ulcer, suddenly enters immortality at the age of
thirty-one in New York City. Valentino came to the
United States from Italy in 1913 and variously worked as a
gardener, dishwasher, dancer in vaudeville and bit part
actor before playing Julio in* The Four Horsemen of
the Apocalypse *(1921). He immediately became the
greatest star of the silent-movie era. His death provokes a
worldwide commotion. There are suicides, riots at his lying
in state, and a queue to see his body that stretches for eleven
blocks.*

Paul *is* feeling better. He has an appetite and hardly any
diarrhea. And his Kaposi is looking fantastic. He shows
me his left foot. The lighter lesions are gone, and the
bigger ones are smaller and paler in colour. Most importantly, he's in a great mood. He's just received a
transfusion and he's feeling strong. On a Saturday
morning, I'm at the hospital with his family. They're
happy and excited: Paul is coming home. He puts on
his street clothes, which he hasn't worn in several
weeks. They fit him loosely. His pants look like they're
empty, and his shirt dangles on his frame. I notice it, we
all notice it, but we all ignore it. Paul walks a bit un-
steadily. There are plenty of arms and smiles to support
him.

1927—The near-bankrupt picture company of Warner Brothers releases The Jazz Singer, *with Al Jolson. In an otherwise silent feature film, they add four songs, incidental music, various sound effects, and a little synchronized speech to replace the title cards. As a result, the story moves along fluidly and the plot becomes gripping. The film is an enormous success. The era of the talking pictures has begun.*

To do something, to pass the time, to assert control, Paul and I rearrange his room. He gives orders and I execute them. We make a circus of it. I huff and puff while lifting a book, then move the bed pretending it's nothing. Paul laughs.

1928 is Paul's year—and today is his birthday—and what a good year it was. Suffrage was extended to men and women equally in Great Britain; the Kellogg-Briand Pact, which outlawed war as an instrument of national policy, was signed in Paris by sixty-three countries; Amelia Earhart flew across the Atlantic, the first woman to do so; Alexander Fleming discovered penicillin, paving the way for the extraordinarily effective practice of antibiotic therapy for infectious bacterial diseases; Ravel's *Bolero* was a universal hit; Canada's Percy Williams was the sensation of the Amsterdam Olympics, winning gold medals in the 100-metre and

200-metre sprints—yes, it could only be a good story for the Roccamatios. Happy birthday, Paul!

1928—The world sees its first animated sound cartoon, Steamboat Willie, by Walt Disney. Its star is a cheerful and mischievous anthropomorphic rodent: Mickey Mouse.

Paul shows me some photos. One is of two boys, fifteenish, sitting in a pile of orange and brown leaves, dressed in jeans and heavy sweaters. They both have wide, slightly demented grins.

"That's James, my best friend in high school, on the left."

He doesn't say who's on the right. The implication is clear: it's Paul himself. I manage to check my gasp. But I stare hard. I try to find one point of resemblance—the hair, the chin, the nose, the glint of the eyes, anything—but there's nothing. Paul Photo and Paul Beside Me are two different people. Paul Beside Me doesn't notice my reaction. Nothing evokes the past, rejuvenates the sick, raises the very dead, like a collection of family photographs. These flashbacks to a healthy past, to a time of boundless energy and clear skin, cheer Paul up. I take in the remaining photos of this hale and hearty ghost in a state of private horror.

We go for a walk, a slow walk. He moves cautiously, dragging his feet lightly, feeling the terrain to avoid any tiring jerks. The summer weather is warm, and there's the sweetest breeze. He's deeply stirred by the expanses of green grass and the leaves rustling in the trees. We sit on a park bench. He can't stop looking about, in a constant state of marvel at Nature. His feelings are intense and radiant. I make 1929 one of our finest stories.

1929—The comic book Tintin au Pays des Soviets *is published, the creation of the Belgian Georges Rémi, better known as Hergé. Another twenty-three volumes of the thrilling adventures of the intrepid reporter will follow. The illustrations are precise, brightly coloured and highly readable, and they are drawn in lines that are long and continuous, without shadowing, a spare yet vivid style pioneered by Hergé that becomes known as "ligne claire," literally, clear line. The world of Tintin will enrapture generations of readers.*

Paul has been home for over two weeks. The house is like a solar system, with Paul as the sun, the centre of it all. In every important room in the house, there is an intercom that is linked to all the other intercoms. The system is on all the time. Every rustle, every cough, every word that the Sun King produces is heard throughout his domain. The kitchen is littered with his culinary whims. Medical journals—he buys *Nature, Scientific American, The New England Journal of Medicine*—lie on bookshelves, on tables, on the floor; his parents secretly loathe these magazines because they make them feel powerless, but he reads them assiduously. His things— a sweater, a half-drunk glass of orange juice, an open book, slippers, an unfinished crossword puzzle, a portable electronic game—are everywhere, left around not because he's spoiled but because he's tired and forgetful.

The routine of the household, as regards his parents and his sister, is nearly military: everything significant is done on time and in a manner that is structured and thorough. The aides-de-camp relay themselves in gently waking their commander-in-chief at precisely midnight so that he can take his AZT. This isn't a sharing of a burden; it's that they all want their turn.

Paul talks of starting his studies again, by correspondence, or, better still, part-time at the University of Toronto. We're enthusiastic. He's thinking of majoring in philosophy and film studies.

1930—The American astronomer Clyde Tombaugh discovers the ninth planet of our solar system, Pluto.

The Roccamatios will be interrupted for a week. Paul and his parents are going to their Georgian Bay cottage.

"It's for my white cells," he tells me. "They don't want to go up. Big spaces, fresh air—it will be good for them."

His optimism seems to be flagging.

1931 is my year, but Paul asks to do it. My story is trite—based on the invention of the game Criss-Cross Words, better known later on as Scrabble, by the American architect Alfred Butts—and I feel sad that day, so I let him have it. Before Paul leaves, he tells me a brief, puzzling story. I feel even sadder afterwards.

1931—The Austrian-born American mathematician Kurt Gödel publishes his Incompleteness Theorem, better known as Gödel's Proof, which shows that within any mathematical system there are propositions that cannot be proved or disproved on the basis of the axioms within that system, and therefore the basic axioms of arithmetic may give rise to contradictions.

Jack and Mary rush Paul back to Toronto. He has abdominal pains that keep him bent in two. They drive him directly to the hospital.

A count of five hundred white cells. Christ. Next to no immunity protection left. He's wide open.

1932—Socialist Realism is declared the official theory and method of artistic composition in the Soviet Union. The building of a classless society becomes the only acceptable theme of any work of art, and the sole criterion by which its worth will be measured. What results are novels and paintings of meticulous political purity—and unremitting mediocrity.

It's a ridiculous thing to put in the balance, but in the balance of things I suppose it's better to be losing a brother than a son. A child dying before a parent, the future before the past—can there be anything more killing to the spirit? It's the ultimate hopelessness, something worse than death: extinction. No one adapts well to disease, but Jennifer is doing it the least badly. As it has with me, Paul's illness has throttled her whistling, youthful insouciance. She is more deliberate, less amused, quieter. She tells me that often at night she worries about the small risks of life and can't fall asleep for them. They terrify her not for her own sake, as you might expect, but for her parents'. With Paul gravely sick, she feels a silent pressure from Jack and Mary: love. She feels that she mustn't at any cost let them down and die. She doesn't use the hair dryer in the bathroom anymore for fear of water and electrocution. She doesn't ride her bicycle anymore for fear of gaping sewer grates and swinging car doors.

I don't want to deal with 1933. In fact, I want to drop the Roccamatios completely. I bring an Oriental game that a friend has recently taught me called go. The rules could not be more simple—you play with black and white beads on a board checkered by vertical and horizontal lines, the aim being to capture more territory than your opponent—but the game is as complex as chess, only more accessible to beginners. I think Paul might get into it. He interrupts me.

"You've forgotten something, haven't you?"

"I don't feel like it today."

"You said it was the only thing that counted."

"Well, maybe—"

"Do you know what happened in 1933?"

"It was the beginning of the New Deal in the United States."

"Try again."

"The rumba is the craze?"

"One more time."

"Welcome King Kong and false eyelashes?"

Paul kidnaps my year. Marco Roccamatio gains majority control over Orlando's group of small shareholders and forces Orlando off the board of directors of the thriving corporation they have been running.

1933—Adolf Hitler becomes chancellor of Germany. The Third Reich is proclaimed from Potsdam. The first

concentration camp is opened on the site of a former am-
munition factory in Dachau, Bavaria.

Since Paul took 1933, I take 1934, his year, and keep
1935. I impose myself. There is no greater, more beautiful thing than a newborn baby and the love one feels
for it. I announce the birth of Lars Roccamatio.

1934—In a poor French-Canadian farmhouse near
Callander, in northern Ontario, the Dionne Quintu-
plets—Émilie, Yvonne, Cécile, Marie, and Annette—are
born and live, the first set of identical quints in history ever
to survive for more than a few hours. The good news amazes
and delights a world in need of good news. Gifts of money,
clothes, food, breast milk, equipment and advice begin to
pour in from all sides. The Red Cross builds a special, ultra-
modern hospital for them across from their farmhouse. But
people aren't just generous; they're also curious. They want
to see these miraculous mites for themselves. In short order
the world begins to move in on the Dionnes. They become
the biggest tourist attraction in Canada. The hospital is ex-
panded and becomes the centre of a complex called "Quint-
land." Tourists come and come and come, as many as six
thousand a day, to see the five through a one-way glass as
they gambol about their special playground. The tourists

spend a total estimated at five hundred million dollars. Across the world, Callander becomes the best-known city in Canada, and real-estate values there soar. Hotels, motels, restaurants and souvenir shops proliferate. Those who can't make the trip to see the Quints in the flesh can see them in their three Hollywood movies, or in the Fox-Movietone newsreels, or on the covers of countless magazines, or in the ads for the many products they endorse. The world wants to know every day how their sweet Quints are doing.

Two days later I go for the excitement of a crisis at Helsinki City Hall.

1935—Conservative Prime Minister R.B. Bennett calls a federal election. Since Confederation his administration has come the closest to being a one-man, quasi-dictatorial show. He guaranteed that he would solve the problems of the Depression. "I'll blast a way through all our difficulties," he said. In 1935, people who can no longer afford gasoline remove the engines from their cars and hitch the cars to horses; they're called "Bennett buggies." In 1935, the Canadian people blast away Bennett. The Conservatives suffer their worst defeat ever, winning only 40 seats in a House of 245. William Lyon Mackenzie King is prime minister again.

Paul is hardly listening to me. I hear a swallowing. I look up from the notes I have made for my story. His eyes are watery and his lips are trembling. I stop.

"Ohhhh," he moans, "I just want to live. I'll give up on any other ambitions." He begins to cry. "I don't c-care if I make nothing of my life. I'll do any l-l-lousy job, anything."

We have been through this before, often, but for some reason, at that moment, I'm not prepared. I panic. I get up from the chair next to his bed. I move towards the door (to get someone?). I sit down again. I get up. I sit on the bed.

"I just want t-t-time."

I want to speak, but the words (what words?) don't come. I want to cry, but I feel that I mustn't so I don't. I stand up. I take hold of the glass of water on his bed-side table.

"It's *so* unfair."

I look at the open curtains (maybe I should close them?). I sit down on the chair.

"I w-wish I had a g-g-girlfriend."

I get up. I put the glass back on the table. I sit on the bed. I put my hand on his hand.

"I can't take it anymore, I just can't t-take it any-more."

I look at the door. I look at his sheets (should I re-arrange them?). I look at him.

"Paul"—I finally manage some words—"Paul, you

can't give up. You've got to hang on till they find a cure. Hundreds of millions of dollars are going into research all over the world, in the US, in France, in Germany, in Holland, here in Canada, everywhere. Scientists are on to this thing like never before for anything else. It's like a huge medical Manhattan Project. They're making new discoveries *every* day. You know that; you're the one who reads all those scientific magazines. Time is on your side, Paul. But you've got to hang on."

He starts to calm down. We talk some more. He falls asleep. I change my story and whisper it to him so that I don't wake him.

1935—The Depression is still on, hard.

I'm stuck in traffic on the 401 as I'm heading home. I can't believe I said that. "Time is on your side." Fuck.

1936—The Spanish Civil War begins, exceptional in its bloodletting ferocity.

Jack just can't manage it. He's a member of that square, hard-working war generation, with a career as straight as a railway track, a salary as hefty as a locomotive, and an emotional reserve like a first-class compartment. He's a man whose happiness operated within a clearly defined structure. When a bomb shattered that structure, he fell apart. He's the one who has adapted the least well to Paul's illness. His emotions are a runaway train. He struggles to cope, to stay in control, to feel useful. He's a fragile man with a hollow look in his eyes and his hair whiter than before. And he's on antidepressants, just like his son.

1937—Japanese forces invading China come to the capital of the Nationalist government. The rape of Nanking ensues. Over the course of six weeks, more than a third of the city is destroyed, approximately three hundred thousand Chinese citizens and surrendered soldiers are killed, and tens of thousands of women are raped.

Paul has received another transfusion. He experiences a moment of strength and—directly related—of euphoria. For 1938 I'm expecting a story inspired by Kristallnacht, the violent pogroms that irrevocably shattered the illusion that Jews might survive in Nazi Germany, but he surprises me.

"You'll like my story," he tells me. And I do.

1938—Lazlo Biro, a Hungarian-born Argentinian, invents the ballpoint pen.

Test, tests, tests. Bad result: lack of oxygen in the blood. Possibly a relapse of PCP. His lungs are fragile and he's afraid; his breathing is quick and shallow. He doesn't want to talk about it, but it's so obviously on our minds. I must tread a fine line.

1939—President Antanas Smetona of Lithuania broadcasts a last speech over the radio, protesting his country's annexation by the Soviet Union, which will be a brutal affair—one quarter of the Gulag will be composed of Lithuanians by the end of the 1940s. Smetona does not want to make his speech in Lithuanian, which no one outside his small country will understand. But he also refuses to speak the tongues of the oppressors, Russian or German. Smetona makes his last speech in Latin.

I walk around the hospital. To prepare myself. Something will come up. I breathe deeply. Amazing remissions have been reported. In some desperate cases of cancer, for example. Why not here? I see people lying in beds. Many of them catch me as I walk by, their heads turned, their eyes wide open. Why are they here? Do they have *it*? I don't want to know. I go down a staircase, am approaching Paul's area. There *are* medical miracles. His system is so young and fit. At the end of a corridor I see a man in his sixties sitting on a chair beneath a window, gently rocking himself back and forth. In his hands he holds a small brown paper bag. Some treat or other, I imagine. He's plainly dressed, and he waits with the meek patience of the underprivileged. Where's your son or daughter, old man? Being examined? Undergoing a test? Or just in a sleep akin to a coma? And what was it? Was it sex? Sharing needles? Looking at the man, I'm overwhelmed by the feeling that he's of no importance. A loser. He could die, his son or daughter could die, and it wouldn't matter to anyone. A funeral without mourners, a few bags of clothes in the corner of a room, an empty bed—that would be it. Nothing left unfinished, no mark made, no significant memories. Behold the suffering of the man of no importance. Behold the solitude of pain. I can't face Paul yet. I walk some more.

1940—Doctor Karl Brandt receives a single-paragraph letter from high up. "Doctors to be designated are to be authorized so that patients considered incurable, as far as can be determined from a thorough and rigorous examination of their state of health, can be granted a mercy killing." Op-

eration T4— (Paul interrupts himself. "Can you believe it? T4, short for Tiergartenstrasse 4, the address in Berlin from which the program was run, and exactly the same name as the cells in the immune system that are attacked by HIV. Isn't that an amazing coincidence?") —*Operation T4 is set in motion. Grafeneck, a home for the physically handicapped run by the Samaritans, is taken over and transformed, the first of six euthanasia centres. 10,654 "incurable" patients will die there, mostly mentally retarded men, women and children, but also the physically handicapped and others considered "useless eaters" by the Nazis. Those who transport the victims wear white coats to keep up the appearance of a medical operation. The killings are done at first by lethal injection or starvation, but then with poison gas administered in rooms disguised as showers. Relatives receive condolence letters, falsified death certificates signed by physicians, and an urn containing ashes. Operation T4 will claim more than 70,000 lives. It ends officially in August of 1941 after protests from church groups, but in fact it continues covertly, killing another 130,000 victims before the end of the war. And the technology, experience and some of the personnel are transferred outside the country, to Poland, for example, where the Nazis have other plans.*

Mary has developed a limited resilience. She has hope.

And when her hope is troubled, when the unthinkable forces itself upon her, she seems to find something within her and, diminished, permanently saddened, still manage to go on. Certainly more than Jack, anyway. Maybe she's religious, I don't know. I am careful never to talk about religion. Who am I to kick at people's crutches?

1941—Marshal Pétain institutes Mother's Day in France.

A lumbar puncture isn't supposed to hurt—it didn't last time—but Paul screams. They have to go at it twice before they get the needle in right. I think I'm cool—I look Jack and Mary in the eyes and I tell them it doesn't really hurt, he's just being over-sensitive, and it's for a good purpose, it'll help in establishing a diagnostic, and it doesn't take long and everything will be all right—I think I'm cool, but when I go to drink, my hand is trembling so much I can't hold any water in my paper cup. I bend over and drink from the tap.

He's back in his room, lying on his side, exhausted. There are bristles on his pale, skull-like face. They stand out individually. I could count them if I wanted to, just below his temples, on his chin, a few more on his upper lip.

"You need to shave," I say, to make light conversation.

He blinks several times before replying. "I'm not shaving anymore."

He doesn't have the strength. But I guess at another reason: because he's been losing the hair on his head and it hasn't been growing back. It's falling out in patches. So now he wants every hair he has.

I feel like bursting into tears. The abandonment of his shaving ritual devastates me. His bony fingers clutch the research notes he's taken. A page lies open on the bed, its title, "The Wannsee Conference," neatly underlined. Fifteen men, senior bureaucrats from the relevant ministries and offices of the Nazi regime, meet in a Berlin suburb to plan the "final solution to the Jewish problem." The Einsatzgruppen, besides being too disruptive to local populations, are unable to keep up with their work. Instead of mobile units of killers, there will be mobile victims. A paradigm shift in policy. As a direct result of the conference, the extermination camps of Belzec, Sobibor and Treblinka are set up, and camps such as Auschwitz, Chelmno and Majdanek increase their efforts, all of them linked by railway lines. The new camps are led and staffed by veterans of Operation T4 and are highly efficient. Belzec, for example, during its ten months of operation, needs an SS staff of only thirty, aided by a hundred Ukrainian prisoners of war, to murder more than six hundred thousand Jewish men, women and children.

Paul is too tired. "I can't," he sighs. "We won't do episode 42. 1942 will be the year of nothingness."

How can any stories be told in the face of this?

"Okay." I feel numb, numb, numb.

1942—The year of nothingness.

The results are in. Paul has a fungus called *Cryptococcus neoformans* in his spinal fluid. There is a risk of meningoencephalitis. The thing could go to his brain. The doctors are going to keep a close watch. At the smallest sign he will be put on amphotericin B and flucytosine. He is strangely calm. I want to forget it all. I want to be a million miles from all this.

1943—Emile Gagnan and Jacques Cousteau invent the first autonomous underwater breathing apparatus. Scuba diving is born.

He puffs out his story weakly. I feel each breath against my cheek. I have so much energy compared to him, so much good health. It feels arrogant. To atone, I do the equivalent of what people who are very tall do: I go about with stooped health.

1944—Antoine de Saint-Exupéry, author of Le Petit Prince, *is shot down over the Mediterranean while on a reconnaissance mission.*

The side effects are too serious: Paul will stop taking AZT. He's happy about it since he will feel better. The announcement stuns me. There's not even the fiction of a cure anymore. I sit beside his bed, trying to contain myself. My throat is tight and I feel heat in my eyes. I have a carefully prepared story, as I always do. Monika Roccamatio is on a train, alone in her compartment, when a dignified older man with a disfigured face and a cane steps in and sits down, and eventually they begin a conversation. But on the spur of the moment I change my historical fact and I change my story. It's the shortest of all Roccamatio stories, a murder. The man strangles Monika. I end the story with an image of the murderer running across a field, escaping. It makes no sense, neither psychologically nor practically. How does the man get off the moving train? I don't explain it. But Paul is pleased.

1945—On August 6, at 8:15 in the morning, the Japanese city of Hiroshima becomes the first city in the world to be struck by an atomic bomb. Nicknamed "Little Boy," the bomb is dropped by the Enola Gay, a B-29 bomber of the US Air Force. The bomb explodes with a blinding flash in the sky, followed by a tremendous rush of air and a deafening rumble of noise. The loudest sounds after that are of falling buildings and roaring fires. The immediate death toll is eighty thousand. Many more will die later of injuries and radiation sickness.

After the hospital I go tramping about the streets of Toronto. I catch the headlines at a newsstand—blood in Sri Lanka, the West Bank, Haiti, Iran, Iraq; the Ku Klux Klan wins an election in Louisiana; a science magazine rings the alarm bell on the health of the oceans—and I am delighted. It sets me off. The world is metastasizing! We are not a viable species! The environment is our worst enemy! Long live the greenhouse effect and acid rain! Down with animals! Let us all rise to the defence of the shrinking of tropical forests and the expansion of the Sahara and the emptying of the oceans. All stocks will be replenished with starvation. Everything will be made better with pollution and human blood. Our mission is a cleansing one: we must scour this earth of anything living. Death is our destiny and destruction our greatest talent. So

hip-hip-hooray for war! Three cheers for poverty! Boo
Amnesty International and the white rhinoceros
and Mother Teresa! In Pol Pot and Shining Path we
trust! LONG LIVE DEATH! DEATH TO INTELLIGENCE!

I look at where I am. I'm on Bloor Street, not far
from Brunswick. I'm in front of a Lebanese greasy
spoon. It's a bright, sunny afternoon. I'm starving. I go
in and order a falafel in pita. I watch the man make it.
I feel something in me start to unwind. I pay and move
on along the street. There's a small supermarket with a
billboard in the entrance. I take in the ads, the lost cats,
the yoga classes, the furniture for sale, the roommates
and drummers wanted, the babysitters on offer, all the
little cries of good will and good deals that are a community billboard. I move on. I come upon a café. All
the beautiful people. The waitress is a blonde dressed
in black with black-rimmed glasses. Sexy. A bum comes
up to me and asks me for some change. I ask him what
he'll spend it on. "Feeding Africa," he replies. I give him
a dollar. He staggers off. I move on. I pause at the display window of a second-hand bookstore. All the interesting books. I go in and buy *The Bridge of San Luis Rey*, by
Thornton Wilder, and a collection of short stories by
the Italian writer Dino Buzzati. I move on, taking in
more stores and more people. The attack wears off
completely. I'm dazzled. All our funny, strange, intricate
ways. I spend the rest of the afternoon wandering
about Bloor Street like a fish poking around a coral reef.

But don't get me wrong: I've merely developed an ability to enjoy catastrophe.

1946—War starts in Indochina between the colonial power, France, and the forces of Ho Chi Minh. The United States will eventually replace the French, and war will continue in Vietnam in one form or another until 1975.

"Look at this," says Paul. His skeletal hand slowly reaches for the top of his head. His fingers select a strand of hair. He pulls. There is a momentary resistance, then the strand comes out. "It makes the funniest little sound. You can't hear it, but it makes the funniest little sound inside my head."

1947—As a prelude to the termination of British rule, India is partitioned to accommodate the fears and aspirations of the subcontinent's Hindus and Muslims. And so India achieves independence and Pakistan is created. But Pakistan is geographically absurd: East Pakistan (now Bangladesh) is more than a thousand miles from West Pakistan. Worse still, the delineation of the new borders through the intermeshed and irreconcilable communities of Bengal and Punjab envenoms an already violent conflict between Hindus and Muslims. There is a massive flow of refugees. Seven to eight million Muslims leave India for Pakistan. About the same number of Hindus make the journey in reverse. Terrible acts of violence take place. More than two hundred thousand people are killed.

Paul's world is shrinking. There can be no question any more of foreign travel. Going home is travel. Leaving his hospital room is travel. He hardly has the strength to walk; he makes it to the bathroom to relieve himself, and even that sometimes is too much of an effort. The edge of his bed is becoming the horizon.

1948—Gandhi is assassinated by a Hindu fanatic.

Jack has always been a local history buff, but since the beginning of Paul's illness it has become his passion. The Family Compact, the Durham Report, the inflexible Sir Francis Bond Head, the great Sir Isaac Brock ("Did you know he came from the Channel Islands?" he asks me)—with these and more Jack is endlessly fascinated and he shares his fascination with me and I listen attentively and ask thoughtful questions, though nothing interests me less than the Family Compact, the Durham Report, the inflexible Sir Francis Bond Head or the great Sir Isaac Brock ("Jersey?" "No, Guernsey.").

I love the man because of his pain. When we talk about the Battle of Queenston Heights or the tragic Tecumseh or the tireless John Graves Simcoe, I come away with the impression that we've been talking about Paul all along.

1949—The People's Republic of China is established, with Mao Tse-tung as its chairman. Chinese independence is at last restored.

Get away, pain.

1950—Under the indifferent eyes of the world, China invades Tibet.

Paul is afflicted with hiccups. These spasmodic jerks drain him completely. He has neither the strength to stay awake nor the peace to fall asleep. He floats in a horrible limbo. The doctors try drugs, then hypnosis. They are worried.

The Roccamatios are interrupted for six days.

When things are at their worst, they suddenly get better. Paul seems to have entered a period of exhausted stability. Miraculously, his hiccupping has stopped. And his diarrhea too, nearly. His lungs—always a worry: one man in the hospital has had seven bouts of PCP—are all right. He's been off alpha interferon since long ago and his Kaposi has spread, but the nearest mirror is far, far away, and he's too tired to care; it's the least painful of his problems. He's under constant perfusion with a hydrating solution of vitamins and minerals, he sleeps a lot, and he rarely gets out of bed. Like a pregnant woman, he has sudden whims for particular foods, but he can hardly hold them down, vomits often.

The year 1950—episode 50—is the last for which Paul takes full responsibility. He can no longer sustain the effort of concentration. He stops reading and he stops creating. Instead he becomes the critical spectator of my imagination. My only respite is that he tires so easily. He falls asleep at any moment, in midsentence sometimes. He doesn't want to sleep; it's his exhausted body that commands it. Often I let him rest, wait till he awakens before I go on with my story, but as the years go by I whisper it, knowing he's sleeping.

1951—The Arab League appeals to its member states to tighten their economic blockade of Israel and, especially, to shut off oil supplies.

Paul finds urinating painful. The doctors check his catheter. There's nothing wrong with it. Some urinary tract infection. Even that simple pleasure is denied him.

1952—The Supreme Court of South Africa invalidates the first elements of the apartheid legislation brought in by Prime Minister Daniel F. Malan. The system of racial segregation has been governing the relations between the races since well before the creation of the Union of South Africa in 1910, but never before in such an intricate, institutionalized way. Shortly after the Court's move, Parliament approves a government-sponsored bill to restrict the powers of the Supreme Court. Malan and his successors, Johannes Strijdom and Hendrik Verwoerd, pursue the construction of apartheid.

Paul doesn't eat anymore. Sometimes he sucks on an ice cube. I arrive eating a chocolate bar, not thinking about it. Paul stares at me, at my fingers, at my mouth. He's not hungry. It's the memory of eating chocolate that makes him crave it. I know that if he takes any, he will vomit. But the look in his eyes! I take a piece, a flake with a little caramel attached to it, and place it on the tip of his pasty tongue. He pulls his tongue in. A few seconds go by. I imagine the flake melting and saliva wetting his mouth. Suddenly he breathes out violently and opens his mouth—nausea! I run my finger over his tongue and remove the offending flake. I put another finger in the glass beside his bed and wet his tongue with a few drops of lemon-flavoured water. He keeps his eyes closed. He's on an edge between nausea and pain on the one side and exhaustion on the other. I wait. He opens his eyes. He's all right. I smile.

"It's bad for you anyway—cavities," I say.

"Pimples too," he replies. He manages a smile.

He's in a good mood. I have prepared two stories. I choose the better one. At the National High School Debating Competition, held in Turku, Georgio Roccamatio triumphs in the debate "Is television good for democracy?" and receives the Kekkonen Award from President Koivisto himself.

1953—Dag Hammarskjöld is elected Secretary-General of the United Nations.

The transfusion is slow, takes time, but Paul's system takes the shock. He feels better.

Then he vomits blood.

"Internal hemorrhage," says the nurse.

I can't stop looking. My eyes won't close or turn away. There is blood and clear liquid on the sheet, on Paul's hand. The nurse puts on plastic gloves; they're a horrible translucent white. Suddenly I'm afraid—of Paul's blood, of Paul himself. I mutter that I'll be back and leave the room. I head for the bathroom. I lock myself in. I start to roll up my sleeves, change my mind and take my shirt off. Someone knocks. I turn my head and look at the door, bewildered. "It's busy. There's no one here," I hush. With hot water and plenty of soap, I begin to wash my hands, my arms, my face. I bring my hands to my face and inspect every square millimetre, searching for the least nick, cut or abrasion.

"There's this"—pause—"burning inside me," Paul whispers when I get back.

I place my hand on the sheet over his chest and gently tap, in sympathy for this burning inside him. In fact, I don't want to touch him. Then at home, for the hundredth time, for the thousandth time, I read that there is no empirical evidence, none at all, that it can be passed on through casual contact.

1954—William Golding's novel Lord of the Flies *is published. It tells the story of a group of schoolboys who are cast away on a Pacific island. At first they get along and work together towards the common good. But soon their relationships degenerate to murderous savagery. Jack rules.*

Not in bed for me, that's for sure. I've thought about it.

Better a bang than a whimper. Better a car crash, with metal screaming and glass exploding, than slowly in bed. Better no goodbyes than slowly. Better a bullet than slowly. Just not in bed, not in bed.

1955—James Dean dies in a car crash.

Paul is in pain. It comes from nowhere. One moment he's fine, the next he's writhing weakly. I can do nothing but wait and watch.

"It h-hurts," he moans (what? where?), fixing me with his eyes. He is dangling over a precipice. Our eyes locked together are like two clasped hands. Should I break eye contact, he will fall to his death. I don't break eye contact.

1956—The Soviet Union invades Hungary to bring to heel a country reluctant to march to the drumbeat of communist totalitarianism. Material damage to the country is heavy, and two hundred thousand refugees flee the country for the West.

Paul is resting. Or at least his eyes are closed. Except for the slight rasp of his breathing, there is silence. I am sitting motionless, my arms crossed, my legs crossed. I want to scream.

He awakes. I smile wanly.

"Hi," I say.

He has chosen this day to talk about God.

"Do you believe in God?" he whispers.

I take note of his tone of voice.

"Yes, I do."

There is a pause.

"I think me too," comes his clipped response. He seems relieved. Tiny beads of sweat cover his forehead. Every time he swallows, he closes his eyes. He has forgotten all our atheistic arguments at university.

"I believe God is everywhere, in every manifestation of life and matter," I add.

"Me too."

"There was never a moment when we weren't with God, nor will there ever be a moment when we aren't with God."

"Yes."

"He cares for us all."

He swallows and falls asleep.

1957—After slanderous accusations that he is a communist are revived in the US Congress, Herbert Norman, Canada's ambassador to Egypt and a renowned scholar of Japan, commits suicide by jumping off the roof of an apart-

ment building in Cairo. McCarthyism adds another Canadian to its list of victims.

I drop by the office of the hospital chaplain. I inform the secretary that Patient Paul, Room So-and-so, Wing So-and-so, would probably appreciate the visit of Charlie Chaplain. "Easy does it," I feel like adding. "We don't want him reading *The Watchtower,* do we?" Instead, I ask what the chaplain's visiting hours are, to make sure I don't bump into him.

"Why don't I eat anymore?" Paul asks. "They should give me a drug that makes me hungry, don't you think? They should feed me, don't you think?"

Before I can answer, he falls asleep. Beside his bed is the latest meal he hasn't touched.

1958—Boris Pasternak declines the Nobel Prize for Literature as a result of harassment by the Soviet government.

This disease. There's nothing left of him. Sharks wouldn't take so much off his frame. Fire couldn't disfigure him more. But it's nothing quick, there's no sudden push into eternity. Only a relentless attrition. He's at the bottom of his bed. He weighs seventy-eight pounds and dropping. He can't walk anymore. He can't control his bladder or sphincter anymore. He labours to breathe. He's as bald as a cue ball. He's so decayed with disease he reminds me of garbage—bad meat, moulding cheese, rotting bread, overripe fruit—yet from this putrefaction a faint, quavering voice clamours its humanity by speaking my name. This disease. It's enough to make me want to pass it on to God.

The rings around his eyes are enormous black circles. His skin is covered in spots, scabs and lesions of every colour, the legacies of tests, injections, transfusions, perfusions and disease. Every shade of blue, black, brown, red, purple, yellow, green, set amidst a complexion that is waxen and translucent. He looks like a dying rainbow. "Tell me, doctor," I feel like saying, "the boy has fever, diarrhea, pneumonia, Kaposi's sarcoma, to name only those with pronounceable names, and you can't do much about it. But could you at least tell me how skin gets *green*?"

1959—The first thalidomide babies are born. Thalidomide, on the market in more than forty countries, is prescribed to pregnant women as a treatment for morning sickness. It is soon found to produce severe deformities in babies, deformities such as phocomelia ("seal limbs," in which the long bones of the arms and legs are absent and the hands and feet grow close to the trunk), malformations of the outer ear,

*fusion defects in the eyes, and the absence of the normal
apertures in the gastrointestinal tract.*

I was hoping to start the new decade with a brighter
story, but Paul is having troubles with his eyes. The
cause seems to be cytomegalovirus. There's nothing to
be done. He's overwhelmed with fear. He asks a nurse
to suffocate him with a pillow. He's given nitrazepam;
it's supposed to help with "acute anxiety."

"I want to get out of here. I hate it here. I'm sick of
being their guinea pig. I want to get out, I want to get
out, I want to get out, I want to get out."

He repeats it twenty, thirty times.

In my hands I hold a piece of paper: "1960—Anne
Sexton publishes her first book of poetry, *To Bedlam and
Part Way Back*. Deeply personal and insistently honest,
the poems chronicle her nervous breakdown and re-
covery in images that are often startling and in a tone
that is sardonic yet vulnerable. She wins immediate ac-
claim." I crumple the paper up. I am stopping the Roccamatios. I want out.

I run into the chaplain as I'm leaving Paul's room.
He's a man in his fifties with perfectly combed white
hair.

"Oh, you're Paul's friend. How are you?" he asks. His
voice is warm. So is his hand. There's nothing religious

about his garb. No cross dangling from his neck, no clerical collar. Only the small black book he's carrying.

"I'm fine."

"It's tough, isn't it?" he says.

"It is."

"Well, I don't want to hold you up." He half turns towards Paul's room. "Would you like to talk about it?"

"I should get going, sir."

By the time I step out of the hospital, I'm so tense I'm trembling. I get to a gravel path. The crunching sound of the pebbles underfoot annoys me instantly. I pound the path with my feet and scream at it. My legs begin to hurt. I run to escape the path. I'm alongside a red brick wall. I stop. My back is to the wall. My fingers feel like hooks. I drop to my knees and scratch the earth, driving the hard black soil under my fingernails. I bring my forehead to the ground and close my eyes. I can feel the ground's rough coolness against my forehead and hairline. I lie very still. I breathe. I lie very still. I breathe. I lie very still. I breathe.

I drive home, crossing those nightmare suburbs of Toronto that devour so much of southern Ontario. I feel relief when I leave Paul, that's the truth—it's an escape from claustrophobia, a vital stretching, a dazed relaxing—but I also feel depressed. When I'm with him, I feel so alive, so brilliantly alive. Away from him, I enter an environment that is cluttered with objects, that assaults me with trivia, commerce and vulgarity, that fills me with numbing boredom. I drive home, crossing those endless nightmare suburbs. I think only of Paul and of the Roccamatios.

There is a sign posted beside the door to Paul's room: "Visitors are informed that Mr. Atsee has gone blind. Could they please identify themselves as they enter." I can't believe my eyes. I head for the bathroom and stay there twenty minutes.

When I go in, Paul is lying there, waiting for me. His eyes are open. They turn my way. I'm nervous. I can't get any words out. Finally I can, and I can't help myself.

"F-f-f-fuck, Paul, you've gone blind."

For the first time ever, I can't help it and I impose my sadness onto his. I break down right in front of him. Great, cracking, uncontrollable sobs.

Who am I to need comfort, but he comforts me.

"Shhh, shhh, it's all"—pause—"right." I can hardly hear him. "Whose turn"—pause—"is it? What year are we?" Pause. "Is it my turn?"

Fuck everything. On the spur of the moment I make up a despairing story.

1961—Dag Hammarskjöld is killed in an airplane crash over the Congo while on a UN peace mission.

"Yes," is all Paul says. He's been receiving morphine shots every twelve hours.

Paul is in a wheelchair. It's Mary's birthday today, and her gift is her son coming home. He's bundled up in a wool cap, a scarf, a sweater, gloves and a blanket, and he's wearing black sunglasses; all that shows of him is his nose and upper lip. We're in the midst of an October Indian summer. I'm not even wearing a jacket. But he's skin and bones. With every jolt of the wheelchair his limbs jerk up like a marionette's.

Last thing I remember from the hospital: I'm walking down the corridor. I notice in a room a trinket on a bedside table. A shiny pink porcelain hand holding a bright red heart. Why is so much about death in bad taste?

Paul is lucid. He's lying on his back in his bed. He's happy to be back home, never wants to go back to the hospital. The room next door has been fixed up for the nurse who is there twenty-four hours a day.

"I'll do"—pause—"one more story," he whispers.

"We're at 1962."

"No." Pause. "You do that. I'll"—pause—"do another year."

"Okay. Which one? Do you want me to help you with the research?"

"No." Pause. "I'll do the year"—pause—"2001." Pause. "That'll make it"—pause—"one hundred years"—pause—"of Roccamatios."

"Great idea, Paul."

"Yes."

He falls asleep, or unconscious, I don't know which. He slips in and out now. I had 1962 all prepared for him, a story based on the publication of Rachel Carson's *Silent Spring*, an exposé on the dangers of chemical pesticides and their terrible cost to the environment.

I enter his room to the strain of "With a Little Help from My Friends." Beatle Paul is curled up on his side, a pillow between his legs. Beatle George, eternally faithful, is lying on the floor beside the bed.

"The year 2001?" I ask.

"Not yet."

What can I say? I must wait. He falls asleep to "Lucy in the Sky with Diamonds."

I put a pen and a pad of paper beside his hand on the bed.

Today it's "A Day in the Life." He's asleep.

Death has a smell. It permeates the house.

"Paul?"

"I'm still"—pause—"thinking."

Jack has bought me a hemp shirt. A few days ago I gave him Mishima's *Sea of Fertility* novels, second-hand, and he's jumped at the opportunity of returning my kindness. He's changed a lot since the beginning of Paul's illness. He's taken an extended leave from his job, and the way he talks about it now, I can't imagine him ever going back to it. His mind and his heart have turned to other things. But he's still so shaky. There's still so much anxiety. He asks what I intend to do with my future. I answer vaguely about travelling and then going back to school. It's not my future I'm worried about—it's his.

"Paul?"

"Not"—pause—"yet."

I walk George H. I like walking dogs. It gives purpose to aimlessness. I can't stand it when people treat their pets like human beings, yet irresistibly I find myself conversing with this creature, brain the size of a lemon. He doesn't seem as bouncy as usual. His tail is low and there's no enthusiasm to his sniffing. I think he may be losing weight. I take a stick, wave it in front of his face and throw it. He watches it sail through the air without moving. When we return home, I ask Mary about George H.'s lack of pep. She looks at him.

"He's not eating much." She gets a treat. "George H.," she commands, staring into his bright black eyes, "one sick person in this house is enough." She throws him the treat. "Eat!" He eats it half-heartedly. I smile. I go down to the basement to cry.

"Paul?"

"I've"—pause—"got it." Pause. "But later."

"Being for the Benefit of Mr. Kite" is playing. I listen to the song. The album starts over. Pulse: 160. Blood pressure: 60 over 30. He's dying. He's sleeping.

George H. has taken to lying on the bed right next to him, though carefully out of his way. He whines quietly. I notice Paul's lips and nostrils are slightly blue. I ask the nurse about it.

"Cyanosis, which means a lack of oxygen in the blood," she tells me.

"Which means PCP."

She nods.

Oh man. All this to end the way it began. A cycle for nothing except protracted agony.

I find something scribbled on the pad, but I can't make anything of it.

He's too weak to move or speak. He just lies there, his eyes blinking once in a while. He's had his morphine three hours before.

"Paul? Paul, it's me."

His eyes blink.

Since my eyes are level with it, I touch his ear. I rub the lobe with my thumb and forefinger. He seems to like it. I get some cotton swabs and I clean Paul's ear, first the outer ear, then, very gently, the inner; a little yellow wax comes out. Paul's mouth trembles into an approximation of a smile.

"Don't worry," I whisper. "It won't be long."

His lips move to make a word. There is no breath to create it. He struggles.

"Two." It barely comes out.

Two. It must be for 2001.

For six days I visit every day. Sometimes he comes to—once Mary even found him sitting up—and he manages to speak a little, but never when I'm there. I ask if he's said anything that was meant for me. There's nothing.

Shortly before three in the morning, George H. shatters the silence. Mary, who has fallen asleep on the sofa beside the bed, awakes instantly. The nurse, who checked on him an hour before, is in the room seconds later, as are Jack and Jennifer. George H. is straddling Paul; his tail is erect, the hairs on his back are standing up, his teeth are bared, and he is barking furiously, barking like he has never barked before.

It would have been episode 63 of the Roccamatios. The year JFK was shot and people cried in the streets. The year I was born.

The news comes to me over the phone. Each word is ordinary, but together they shock me breathless. I head over to their home.

I'm sitting in the hallway, outside his room. All is quiet. Someone touches my shoulder. It's the nurse. A friendly, efficient woman in her fifties. She sits down beside me.

"I'm sorry about your boyfriend."

I don't react.

"He came to at around ten last night. We talked for a minute or two. He asked me to write something down and give it to you. It wasn't very clear, you know, but I think I got it right."

She hands me a neatly folded piece of paper.

For some reason I'm amazed at her handwriting. Nice round clear letters, with the i's precisely dotted and the t's neatly crossed. Incredibly legible. Christ, if you compare it to my handwriting, so jagged and messy.

"Could you keep this a secret, please?" I ask her.

"Sure."

She stands up. She's looking down at me. There's a moment of silence.

Then, just like that, she runs her hand through my hair.

"You poor boy," she says.

2001—After a reign of forty-nine years, Queen Elizabeth II dies. Her reign has witnessed a period of incredible industrial expansion and increasing material prosperity. In its own blinkered and delusional way, the second Elizabethan age has been the happiest of all.

Sorry, it's the best I could do. The story is yours.

Paul

The Time I
Heard the Private
Donald J. Rankin
String Concerto
with One
Discordant Violin,
by the American
Composer
John Morton

I WAS YOUNG (I am young: I'm twenty-five—it was just last October, October of 1988) and I was down in Washington, District of Columbia, visiting an old high-school friend. I had never been to the United States before. My friend works in the management-consulting arm of an accounting firm called Price Waterhouse, in their aviation practice. He's very bright—he went to the John F. Kennedy School of Government at Harvard—and now he makes good money. But the point is, he was busy at work during the day, and the weather was sunny and mild. So I visited Washington. I visited the public parts of the city, the parts where single buildings take up entire city blocks and have their own postal codes and where you must walk and walk and walk until you find their monumental entrances, the parts where even the green grass speaks of confidence, for only a nation supremely confident of its values would have such vast, open lawns at its heart, the parts of the city where there is much to look at and admire.

Then I went further afield, risked my life, some would say. For several days running, I went into the private parts of the city, those that were never meant for show. I walked up streets of no historic distinction and down their alleyways. I patronized corner stores and greasy spoons. I examined storefronts and bus shelters, newspaper boxes and ads on utility poles, boarded-up buildings and untended yards, graffiti and the mounds of garbage beneath them, cracked sidewalks and laundry hanging to dry from windows. I spoke about politics with a homeless man on a park bench next to a shopping cart holding all his earthly possessions. Within sight of the dome of the Capitol—it seemed to float in the air like a hot air balloon—I came upon a dead rat. I found everything interesting because everything was a part of Washington, and Washington was new and foreign to me. For a rich and powerful city, the capital of the world in some ways, it has a lot of run-down parts. Whole areas where the painting and fixing up is put off to tomorrow the way people put off exercising and eating better.

I was walking back home one afternoon when a sign caught my eye. MERRIDEW THEATER, it said, printed in an arc across a store window. Some of the letters were scratched out, with only their outline left. It was more like MER I EW T EA R. In the bottom left-hand corner of the window was a small, red-and-white cardboard sign: Mel's Barbershop. Through the window, in what was, presumably, once a part of the theatre, I could see two barber chairs. A black man was sitting in one and another black man—Mel?—was cutting his hair. The Merridew was no more, it seemed. But to the right of the door was a small display case with a paper inside. A sign of life? I moved closer.

Special Concert at the Merridew Theater
THE MARYLAND VIETNAM WAR VETERANS'
BAROQUE CHAMBER ENSEMBLE
plays
ALBINONI
BACH
TELEMANN
and the world premiere of
THE PRIVATE DONALD J. RANKIN STRING
CONCERTO
WITH ONE DISCORDANT VIOLIN,
BY JOHN MORTON
8 p.m., Thursday October 15th, 1988
COME ONE, COME ALL!
Tickets: only $10 at the door

That was tomorrow night.

Perfect. Another aspect of Washington to explore, another convolution in its brain, another chamber in its heart. Not that I was particularly interested in the Vietnam War. It was a foreign war, an American trauma. I had seen the movies and documentaries on it, had read the odd long article, I knew it sank Lyndon Johnson's presidency—but it remained folkloric to me, like the Second World War, something long ago that was now the stuff of garishly coloured visuals and hero movies. Nor would I be going for the announced fare. I could listen to Bach any time I wanted on my stereo. It was the idea of a spectacle, of a *happening,* that attracted me to this concert at the Merridew Theater, not an evening of classical music. Although this Rankin Concerto—with One Discordant Violin, whatever that was—was intriguing. I would ask my friend if he wanted to come. I had hardly seen him since I had arrived.

But Price Waterhouse was about to close a deal with Texas Air's unions, and the City of New York had responded earlier than expected to a PW proposal to do work at JFK and LaGuardia airports. He was busy.

So there I was the next evening, at about five to eight, alone in front of the Merridew Theater. I tried the door. It opened. To my left was the door to Mel's Barbershop. Straight ahead lay a corridor, at the very end of which I could see a piece of paper taped to the wall. I walked down the corridor past several closed doors. THIS WAY, said the paper, with an arrow pointing left to a door. I went through.

I found myself in the lobby of the Merridew. To my right was a series of double glass doors—the main entrance to the theatre. I suppose the doors gave onto a street perpendicular to the one I had just come off, but I couldn't tell: the double doors were all boarded up. Some of the glass panes were broken. Against the doors lay a very long, rolled-up carpet. I noted the ticket booth across the lobby; its windows were grey with dust. In fact, great portions of the lobby were grey with dust. It was unmistakable: the theatre had closed down, was abandoned, and I had just entered through the back door, where the offices had once been. But the lights were on, and the doors I had come through were unlocked, and I was certain I had read the time and the place of the concert right. I stepped forward. Immediately I noticed the table that was set next to a large pillar. Two men, one black, one white in a wheelchair, were sitting behind it. They were looking at me. The word "trespassing" popped into my mind.

"Hello. There *is* a concert here tonight, isn't there?"

"There is, " said the black man.

"Oh, good." I approached the table. "I'll have one ticket, please."

"That'll be ten dollars."

I gave my ten US dollars to the white man in the wheelchair. He put the bill in the cigar box in front of him, carefully flattening it out against the other bills, and gave me a program.

"Am I too early?"

"No, you're right on time," replied the black man. "Just take a chair and sit where you want."

With a casual wave of the hand he directed my attention to a stack of orange, plastic folding chairs. I went over and picked one up. But I didn't know where I was supposed to go with it. Was the concert outside somewhere? In a parking lot? The weather was about warm enough.

"That way." This time he was pointing to the doors at the back of the lobby.

"Thank you."

As I was nearing the doors, I turned and looked about.

"Fixing things up?" I said.

"Beg your pardon?"

"Are they renovating the theatre?"

"No, they're tearing it down."

"Oh."

A covert operation, this Vets' Ensemble, I thought, as I pushed the door and entered the theatre. I climbed a few steps.

As the door swung to and fro behind me, I stood stock-still and astounded. The man had meant it; they really were tearing the place down. There was a multitude of details to take in. It was a large theatre, with balconies and other elements of architectural ambition. But to start with the most practical detail to arrest me: there wasn't a single fixed seat in the house. Every row had been torn out, without care for the damage done. The result looked like something from the First World War: between curving rows of dark and dusty green carpeting—the battlefields of France—ran channels of broken grey cement, with chipped holes, cement flakes and rusted bolts sticking out—the soldiers' trenches. There was a musty smell in the air, no doubt coming from the intricate blotches of yellowish brown, black-streaked mould that covered the walls of the place and made them look like huge medieval maps tracing the spread of the Black Death. And at the foot of the wall opposite me, beyond the trenches from Vimy Ridge and beneath the pestiferous towns of the Middle Ages, stretching nearly the entire length of the wall, were the remains of classical Greece: a great number of smashed up, faux-antique plaster sculptures. Arms, legs, heads, torsos, shields—it was an evenly spaced butchery of gods.

I made my way into this shamble of civilizations. There was an audience of about one hundred and fifty people. Mostly men. A few in wheelchairs. One man had a dog, a German shepherd. Conversations were going on quietly. I seemed to be the only person who had come on his own. I found myself a space, cleared away some cement flakes with my foot, and set my chair down. I took notice of the stage. It had been swept and was well lit. At the centre of its glow was a crescent of twelve orange seats and twelve stands, with a thirteenth stand in the middle. At least art would have a neat and tidy space. I examined the program.

The left side:

Tomaso Albinoni: Concerto in B flat, opus 9, No. 1
Concerto in G minor, opus 10, No. 8
Johann Sebastian Bach: Concerto No. 6 in B flat major
Concerto in A minor
Concerto in D minor
Georg Philipp Telemann: Concerto in G major
intermission
John Morton: The Private Donald J. Rankin String Concerto
with One Discordant Violin
(World Premiere)

The right side:

The Maryland
Vietnam War Veterans'
Baroque Chamber Ensemble
is
Stafford Williams; conductor
Joe Stewart; first violin
Fred Bryden, Peter Davis, Randy Duncan,

Zbig Kerkowsky, John Morton, Calvin Paterson; violins
Stan "Laurel" Mackie, Jim Scotford; violas
Lance Gustafson, Luigi Mordicelli; cellos
Luke Smith; double bass

Special thanks to: Fife, Jeff, Marvin, Frenchie;
Don Beech and the music department of
Morrow Heights Junior High School;
the Mayor's Office, City of Washington, DC;
Marvelous Marvin; and especially, for kicking us
when we needed kicking, Billy.

The back of the program was an ad for Marvelous Marvin's Pizzeria.

So the composer of the Rankin Concerto was a member of the ensemble. And I would have to check out Marvelous Marvin's. I folded the program and put it in my breast pocket. I looked about the Merridew again, delighting in my disbelief.

At a quarter after eight, the two men from the ticket table came in. One, cash box on his lap, wheeled down to the front, while the other sat near the doors. A head popped out briefly from the edge of the stage. The lights went out a moment later. Only the stage remained lit.

Thirteen men in tuxedos, twelve with instruments, walked on stage. Immediately there were shouts and cheers as if we were at a sporting event. The men smiled, bowed and sat down, except for Williams. I tried to figure out which one was John Morton. The violins were seated on the left. I reckoned Joe Stewart, as first violin, was in the first seat. Now, do violinists sit in alphabetical order, or is there some sort of hierarchy? If they obeyed the alphabet, John Morton was a white man in his forties, somewhat overweight, with pudgy facial features and long, slicked-back hair that curled at the ends. That was violin number six.

The musicians adjusted their stands and tuned their instruments. Stafford Williams turned to the audience. He was a towering giant of a black man. In a deep, booming voice, he said, "The fire marshal of Washington, DC, has instructed me to tell you that there cannot be any smoking during this event. The permit—"

"You mean we can't waltz with Mary Jane?" somebody shouted.

Everyone laughed. "That's right," replied Williams. He raised his hands; the audience hushed instantly. "Albinoni's Concerto in B flat," he announced.

He turned around. He raised his right hand. Bows went to strings.

A moment's pause.

His hand dropped, and my ears were invaded.

It was the sheer volume that dumbfounded me. One second the Merridew was collapsed in silence; the next, great billows of music were blowing through it. It was as if the house were an empty lung that was sud-

denly filling with fresh air. An immaterial something—
meandering and sliding and oh so beguiling—had surrounded us, taking over the entire space, right down to
the last crack and crevice. I was certain every mouse
and cockroach in the place was also transfixed. And all
this produced by those small, brown objects.

I took in the consonance of things: the way the
bows moved together, the way the hands climbed up
and down the fingerboards like so many spiders working on their webs, the way Williams's movements were
translated into their musical equivalent, the way Stewart would lead, and then be followed. Such ability, such
agility—how do they do it? What would it mean to be
able to do that with one's hands?

Albinoni's Concerto in B flat was in three parts. I
know nothing about music, so I cannot describe it
properly, but the first part of the concerto was very
lively, like a dance. I could imagine couples flying in circles, with gorgeous dresses swishing about. The melody
went up and down, up and down, up and down, and
then in splendid spirals, then up and down again, and
then it ended. The notes raced along in a lovely, swift
way. The second part was more like a stately straight
line, sober and slow moving, but with a climbing
grandeur, as if the line were following the ridge of a
high mountain, where the air is sharp and rare. The
third part was like the first, with ups and downs and
spirals, though slower.

What a strange, wondrous thing, music. At last the chattering mind is silenced. No past to regret, no future to worry about, no more frantic knitting of words and thoughts. Only a beautiful, soaring nonsense. Sound— made pleasing and intelligible through melody, rhythm, harmony and counterpoint—becomes our thinking. The grunting of language and the drudgery of semi- otics are left behind. Music is a bird's answer to the noise and heaviness of words. It puts the mind in a state of exhilarated speechlessness.

During the Concerto in B flat, music was my think- ing. I don't recall any words, only a light and fluctuat- ing state of being-in-music.

When the concerto ended, there was clapping and there were cheers. The Maryland Vets' Ensemble stood up, bowed and sat down again. Williams's hand went up, went down, and there was music again; this time it was Albinoni's Concerto in G minor.

It was striking too, but I don't remember it clearly. The truth is, my attention started to wander. Words started cropping up in my mind. I started thinking about Texas Air Corporation. My friend had explained the case to me in all its complexity. Texas Air was based in Houston, and its president was a man named Frank Lorenzo. It wasn't an airline company itself—my friend called it a holding company—but it owned two airlines: Eastern and Continental. It seemed that Eastern, based in Miami, was experiencing serious financial difficulties. It was embroiled in a dispute with its three unions over wages, working conditions and retirement benefits, and it was steadily losing customers. To reduce losses and generate cash to finance operations, Texas Air was shrinking the airline by selling assets and trimming its staff and routes. For example, it had sold its profitable New York-to-Boston and New York-to-Washington shuttles to Donald Trump for 365 million dollars. But the unions were claiming that this strategy was—claps and cheers. The Concerto in G minor was over.

The Maryland Ensemble got up, bowed, left the stage, came back, and resumed their seats. Williams's hand again commanded the attention of the audience, and music flowed once more. I took out the program and read it by the light of the stage. Bach's Concerto No. 6 in B flat major. The first part was led by the violas, Mackie and Scotford. It was a swaying, ascending melody that rose like two mountaineers tied to each other with a rope: Mackie would move the piece forward, then Scotford would catch up and pass him, at which point Mackie would redouble his efforts and surge ahead, and so on. The other instruments did background work, the hubbub at a party that allows two people to be intimate. But the second part of the concerto was ponderous to my ears, and it lost me.

The unions were claiming that this strategy was a sham, that the sale of the shuttle routes and the wage-cut demands were all part of Texas Air's plans to dismantle Eastern through bankruptcy, which would allow it to break contracts and slash wages and reconstruct the airline as a non-union carrier. Lorenzo had done exactly that in 1983 with Continental. The dispute was bitter and protracted, a real war, and the publicity hadn't done Eastern any good. Travel agents were reporting that some customers didn't want to travel with Eastern anymore, even when its flights were the most convenient. If the dispute went on much longer, a matter of months some analysts were saying, the airline might no longer—another burst of applause. No. 6 had slid to an end. The Concerto in A minor was up next. I remember that Stewart was kept busy by it.

The whole thing was a mess. Price Waterhouse was hoping to get a contract with the unions, and every night my friend brought home piles of documents and worked till two in the morning. During breaks he would tell me about developments—Lorenzo's latest move, some judge's ruling, the threats of the AFL-CIO—and I would tell him where I had been that day and what I had seen.

Merridew. I wondered who Merridew was. Wasn't he the Secretary of State who had bought Alaska from the Russians? No, that was Seward. Seward's Folly it was called, not Merridew's.

I looked about the theatre. Five days ago I was in my university town, Roetown, not happy but not particularly unhappy, just wondering what to make of life—and here I was in Washington, DC, listening to some war vets play Bach in a theatre that looked like Beirut. After a number of interruptions, I would be going back to school in January and finally getting my philosophy Bachelor's. What after that? What should I do, where should I head? I considered various career options. In what oyster did I want to be a grain of sand?

The A minor ended. I checked the program. It was the turn of the D minor. It had some exquisite violin parts, but I couldn't help thinking. Looking at the program again, I noticed that the Maryland Ensemble had used colons between the composers and their concertos, but semi-colons between the musicians and their roles or instruments. I was reminded of Joseph Conrad. Conrad has marvellous punctuation. There's one example I'll never forget. It's from Conrad's first novel, *Almayer's Folly*. Almayer has been working in the desolation of a remote corner of the Malay Archipelago for twenty years. He hates it, has hated it all along, but has kept at it because he wants to return to Europe a rich man for the sake of his beautiful, half-caste daughter Nina. As he puts it, "I wanted to see white men bowing before the power of your beauty and your wealth." But twenty years in the archipelago have been twenty years of disappointments, humiliations and poverty. The last straw comes when Nina, who has never known anything but this tropical place and is happy here, chooses to marry her Malay lover, Dain, in spite of her father's objections. She'll never be going to Europe. Almayer is devastated. He has lost it all. His ceaseless efforts have yielded nothing but failure and ruin. Yet it didn't have to be this way. Almayer feels that time and again he nearly made it. Fortune, success, glory—nearly achieved, nearly, but for some misfortune, some small error:

He looked at his daughter's attentive face and jumped to his feet, upsetting the chair.

"Do you hear? I had it all there; so; within reach of my hand."

What a brilliant use of semicolons. Admire the construction: five words fore and aft balanced upon a fulcrum of a single word that carries all the weight and tension of the sentence. An ordinary writer would have used commas to surround that fulcrum. Dashes would have done the job. But semicolons, by isolating the "so" without making it parenthetical, give the word a real impact. Their bottom halves curl like the fingers of two hands raised in frustration, their periods glare like two desperate eyes, and the word held between them shouts with the wretched hopelessness of twenty years that have added up to nothing. The punctuation of this sentence is deliberate, forceful and dynamic. It is the punctuation of a true master.

At last the D minor was through. This concert was endless. I checked the time. Only 9:33 p.m. Still the

Telemann to go before intermission. The thought of leaving then entered my mind. But I convinced myself to stay. Come on, I thought, the composer of the next concerto is here, right in front of you. And what's a "discordant" violin? It could be very good. I remembered a Dutch violinist I had heard in Montreal. His piece had been pure noise, a mix of long monotones interrupted by head-shaking frenzies of screeching notes and frantic plucking. Not a trace of melody or rhythm, only an assault on the senses that had sent a number of spectators packing. I had loved it. So full of life. And there was that Ukrainian-Canadian composer I had seen in Roetown. He played what he called "continuous music"; his fingers moved like waves up and down the piano, the melody evolving ever so slowly. It was mesmerizing. Yes, this Rankin Concerto could be very good. Why, I wouldn't miss it for anything.

The second part of the Telemann was very energetic, and my mind was speechless. The piece ended with a flourish. There was clapping, whistling and hooting. The ensemble members bowed several times and left the stage with their instruments. The house lit up.

Intermission, at long last.

A shout startled me. "I GOT MICHELOB, I GOT OLD MILWAUKEE, I GOT CORONA, AND I GOT LONE STAR." It was the man at the doors. He had produced five big blue coolers. His compadre with the cash box quickly wheeled up to him and parked himself behind the coolers. They started selling their beers. In my Canadian mind I asked myself, *Is this legal?* I got up to stretch my legs. I walked through the war trenches and had a look at a particularly vivid splotch of mould on the wall. It looked very much like a medieval town. I wondered whether I would see a burgher bug crawling about a street, the poor thing worried about those strange bumps beneath its armpits and the fever afflicting it since this morning. Don't they say the Black Death claimed one third of medieval Europe's population? I reached up to touch the wall; the wallpaper was so rotted I could have torn a strip off.

Glancing down at the fractured sculptures at the foot of the wall, I noticed Athena's helmeted head. She was the only one I recognized. The other remains were anonymous Greek emblems of male and female physical perfection. The fact that heads, limbs and torsos were severed from their constituent parts—the edges sharp, the exposed plaster so rough—gave a harrowing quality to their beauty. I bent down and turned a head my way. Its gaze, intended as blank, was now tragically stoic. I was tempted to try and reassemble the sculptures.

The members of the audience were standing in groups and talking. I felt like an uninvited guest at a party. I returned to my seat and hunkered down, losing myself in mental trivia.

Then I felt it, after close to forty minutes: I felt the

tension in the air. Everyone had sat down again and the talking had stopped. The expression on all the faces I could see was serious. It dawned on me: Albinoni, Bach and Telemann—they were there only to kill time. Everyone was here for the Rankin Concerto.

The lights went out.

Stafford Williams walked on stage, followed by the other musicians. I could hear the creaking of the floorboards. Eleven men sat down, two remained standing. The alphabet theory was correct: John Morton was who I thought he was. He walked over to Williams and whispered a few words to him. Williams nodded. Morton stationed himself to the conductor's left. He raised his violin to his shoulder, tilted his head to anchor it, and lightly ran his fingers over the fingerboard. Then he lifted his right hand to bring the bow just above the strings. An image flashed in my mind: the Sistine Chapel, the Creation of Adam, God's hand reaching for Adam's—the electric gap between their fingertips. Morton looked to Williams. Williams brought his right hand up. In a single, matching motion the others brought their bows into position. Morton had his eyes on the right hand. The hand came down—and how can I describe what I heard?

If music were colour, the theatre would have become a kaleidoscope of colours. I could have described the sombre blue that poured from the double bass, the blue and green that flowed from the violas and cellos, the yellow and orange that streamed from the violins. And especially I could have described the red and black that cried from Morton's violin. If music were colour and I were a chameleon, I would have changed colours forever, I would be indelibly streaked in the colours of the Rankin Concerto.

I could describe the music with my deaf eyes. There was nothing to be seen except the stage. The rot and decay of the theatre disappeared. The audience disappeared. Only the stage existed, and on that stage, only John Morton. I saw an ugly man become beautiful. The ugly man had protruding eyes and a piggish face and a belly that bulged against his rented tuxedo shirt. The beautiful man was crumpled over, disfigured, visibly trembling. The beautiful man was a failure. I saw ugliness become suffering become beauty.

The Rankin Concerto wasn't long, not ten minutes, and they didn't play it right, nor did they finish it the way they were supposed to, but during those few minutes everything in my life that is waste, torment and drivel was swept away—the clouds parted—and I beheld the sublime.

It started formally, in the manner of a court dance; imagine the dancers as they move slowly and precisely, each knowing what to do and what his or her partner will do. But shortly it tumbled into a lively and logical melody that ran so naturally I could nearly predict it, could imagine completing it had it been left unfinished in my care. The concerto then began to climb in tight spirals to very high notes. It stayed on these high notes through turn after turn, vacillating like a spinning dish at the end of a stick in a Chinese acrobats' show. From that height it crashed down into the lively melody again, crashed down the way a spring torrent crashes down, with thunder, exuberance and abandonment.

Morton carried most of the piece. He would often break away to turn out curls of pioneer notes. The ensemble, in hot, relentless pursuit, would swell and repeat these notes. The melody was intricate; Morton's left hand jumped and trembled all over the fingerboard while his bow see-sawed madly. And right from the start he was making mistakes. This I must make clear, it is capital: the Rankin Concerto was poorly played. Even my uneducated ears could detect notes that were smudged or not quite right, or a slowing down in the playing because Morton couldn't keep up. But it didn't detract. On the contrary. The full force of the Rankin Concerto was expressed through Morton's inept playing. His every false note hinted at impregnable perfection, his every falter was liberating. This was like no music I had ever heard before. There was no robotic flawlessness here. Like punk rock, like Jackson Pollock, like Jack Kerouac, it was truly human, a mix of perfect beauty and cathartic error.

The music slowed down. The violas and cellos put forth steady blue notes. The concerto seemed to be catching its breath, much as Morton was. He wiped his left hand against his jacket and licked his lips. His expression was strained.

The ensemble revived and played deep, tugging under-notes.

Morton started again. Here language will fail me. There are probably technical terms that define precisely what Morton did, but if there are, I don't know them. How does one say in the jargon of musicology that my soul was pulled out of me and thrown up in the air, to be tossed about by the music? How does one say that I breathed, that I existed, in harmony with the ups and downs of those notes? And what kind of notes are they that gyre and waver, one moment trembling like a whisper, as if about to fade from existence, the next clawing at the air like a tiger, each one, flawed or perfect, of a delicacy that hurt? What kind of notes both elevate and cast down, exalt and crush?

In the midst of this blessed suffering came the discordant violin. It didn't last thirty seconds. The ensemble was producing a large body of blue, green and orange middle notes, hovering notes, when Morton suddenly began climbing and diving above and below them with high red notes and low black notes. If sound can convey feeling, then this was it, this was great emotion made aural, this was emotion perfectly translated from the keenly felt to the heard to the keenly felt again. And what I felt at that moment, the emotion with which I was stricken, was terrible grief, of a kind throbbing and overwhelming. For those few seconds, I was thrust into a state of *agony*.

The discordant violin ended with the ensemble abruptly switching to uniform, oscillating notes. It was an unexpected break, like a sudden attempt at regaining composure. But Morton had lost all composure—he was making mistakes continually—and then he simply gave up and stopped playing. His hands dropped to his sides, the left holding both bow and violin in a cross shape, and he stood there, face cast down. The rest of the ensemble soon lost control too, despite Williams's valiant attempts to steady the course. The music was there, recognizably; it began to stray; then it was lost completely. The house filled with a grey blur of sound. The musicians abandoned the struggle, first violin Stewart last. The silence was sudden.

I felt as though I had been let go, as though I had fallen back into myself on my seat. My heart was pounding and I was breathing through my mouth. I wanted to bring my hands out towards him, Morton. It was there, I had seen it, I had felt it: great, powerful beauty.

The silence lasted. There was no clapping. Emotion was on the surface of everything. I felt that if I had touched the walls or the floor, they would have shuddered.

The house lights came on. I didn't move. Walls in

my ways of being had been pulled down and I was experiencing an amazing feeling of freedom. I felt emptied, opened, transfigured.

I became aware of various sounds. Sudden intakes of breath. Bodies moving in chairs. The whine of the German shepherd. Audience members began to leave; they did so quietly, as if we were in a church. The musicians departed the stage one by one. Morton was the third to go.

I didn't move. I looked about. The Merridew Theater had changed. It was no longer a ruin: it was a magnificent temple.

The black man from the ticket table came in. I was the last spectator in the house. He noisily started stacking the orange chairs. I decided to help him. After stacking about fifteen chairs, and feeling I had earned a bit of conversation, I said to him, "That was beautiful."

He stacked four chairs before replying. "Yeah."

I stacked another five. "Has he recorded anything?"

"Nope."

Another five. "Has he composed anything else?"

"Nope. Only time he got his act together."

Another five. "Is he married?"

A stupid question. I don't know why I asked it. It was the first question I could think of that wasn't related to music. Something confused in my mind about his relationship with the world.

"Is he *married*?" the man repeated, looking at me for

the first time. "Yeah, he's married. Her name's Johnnie Walker."

I thought I better let the man be. I looked about the theatre one last time. "Thank you. See you," I said. He didn't reply. I slipped out.

At the table in the lobby, the man in the wheelchair was counting money. He looked up and nodded. I waited till he had finished counting a stack of ten-dollar bills.

"That was beautiful," I said.

He smiled. "Wasn't it? But I wish they'd finished it." He was friendlier. He had a Southern accent, and a high-pitched voice, strained, as if he had a sore throat.

"I thought it was great just the way they played it."

"Yeah, yeah, I agree with you totally. It was great like that, too."

"Has he composed much else?"

"Oh yeah, definitely. But nothing quite as *finished* as this one."

He started counting five-dollar bills.

"Good night?"

"We should have enough to cover the tuxes and the chairs."

"Do you always play here?"

"No, we usually play in a high-school auditorium, but this time we decided to go for a real theatre, what with John's concerto. That was the world premiere, you know."

"I read that. You should try to get it recorded some-where. I mean, it was really something."

"Yeah, we should. But it's tough, it's tough. We're not professional, and classical music is a hard sell. But Billy's going to try again."

He started counting a stack of dollar bills. I heard behind me the sound of a throat clearing. I turned.

It was John Morton. He was dressed in baggy green workpants and a shirt to match. He was holding a vio-lin case in one hand and a plastic bag in the other. I had seen him on stage, up there, but to have him right in front of me—I was awestruck. I moved to the side.

"Hi, Fife," he said. He had a light American accent, not far from a Canadian one. Fife stopped counting.

"Hey, big guy. Great concert, man, great concert."

"I don't think so," Morton replied.

"What are you talking about? We were just saying it was great, weren't we?" Fife looked at me.

"Yeah, it was. I've never heard anything like it. It was incredible."

"But I didn't finish it. I—"

"Didn't matter one bit," interrupted Fife. "It was beautiful the way it was."

I nodded vigorously. I couldn't take my eyes off his big face.

Morton shook his head dubiously. "Can I give you this?" He held up the bag; in doing so he put the violin case on the table. The bag had a picture of a fox dressed in a tuxedo on it and the words Tuxedo Town Rentals above it. I eyed the violin case. I had a vision that it contained a small brown animal, very dangerous and aggressive except in the hands of its trainer.

"Sure," said Fife. He took the bag and opened it. "Everything's in here?"

"Yeah."

"Good." Fife dropped the bag beside his wheelchair, next to other bags from Tuxedo Town Rentals.

"Thanks. Okay, I gotta run." Morton half-turned. He passed his hand through his hair.

"John, it was great," Fife repeated.

"Where's Billy?"

Fife pointed at the theatre doors.

"What's he doing?"

"Probably destroying the chairs."

"What did he think?"

"Well," said Fife in a long drawl, "at one point I thought he was going to rip my right wheel off, so I guess he liked it."

"Really?"

"John, trust me. That's the way it should be—so beautiful you can't finish it."

Morton nodded. "Meeting tomorrow, right?"

"That's right."

"Okay. Night, Fife. Thanks."

"See you tomorrow, Johnny boy. Now you be proud of yourself and take it easy tonight."

Morton nodded again, to him and to me, and walked off. I watched him go. Fife started counting change. Did I dare or didn't I? It was too late. No, it wasn't. It was. It wasn't. Suddenly I decided: it wasn't.

"I have to go. I thought it was amazing—in fact, it was the best concert I've been to in my life. Goodbye."

"That's great. Thanks a lot. Goodbye."

I pushed the door and raced down the corridor. Just as I got to the street I saw Morton in a car pulling away from the curb and heading to my right. It was a big rectangular box of a car that made a noise like a tugboat.

Without a moment's hesitation I began running after it. I don't know what I was thinking; I don't normally chase after cars on foot (or in another car, for that matter). Morton quickly disappeared around a corner. But thanks to red lights, slow turning, leisurely driving and really hard running, worthy of the most automobile-hating dog, I managed to follow him all the way to where he was going, which was miles away. I don't know what cutthroat neighbourhoods I sprinted through. People who saw me coming flattened themselves against walls. When I got to Morton's parked car, he was nowhere in sight. Gasping for breath, I collapsed on the sidewalk. I was drenched in sweat, my heart was jumping around in my chest, and my legs were killing me. "Christ, all this for nothing," I panted.

After several minutes I started feeling better. I got

up and walked around the car. Where did he live? Was there a way to find out?

Then I saw him. Across the street. He was inside a bank. It was closed, of course—it was past eleven at night—but some lights were still on. Morton was walking in front of the counters. He was pushing a cart that held an open garbage bag and carried brooms, brushes, rags and cleaning products.

He was a janitor.

He pushed the cart to the middle of the floor and took out a Mr. Clean bottle. He drank two gulps from it. After that he found a broom, a soft and flat orange thing, and swept the marble floor. When he had finished, he pushed the cart against the counters and disappeared to the right.

He reappeared, wheeling in a heavy floor polisher, the kind with a large round buffing pad in the front and two small wheels at the back. He plugged it in and proceeded to polish the floor. I couldn't hear the machine, but I knew it made a moderately loud humming sound. Morton calmly manoeuvred it in a slow, to-and-fro motion. There looked to be a certain meditative satisfaction to what he was doing.

What did I have to say to the man? Nothing but expressions of gratitude and admiration. Might he take it wrong? Find me annoying? He took a break to drink from the Mr. Clean bottle. Was he a happy drunk—or a mean drunk?

Soon enough he had polished the entire floor. He unplugged the machine and began wrapping the cord around it.

I had to make a decision. It was late, dark, I'd come this far—what could be the worst that could happen?

I crossed the street, stepped up to the window and knocked on the glass.

Morton turned his head. His puzzled face was on me. He looked for a second, then went back to what he was doing.

I knocked once more.

He turned a second time. I pointed to my right, to the bank's front doors.

He turned his palms out and shrugged.

I brought my left hand level with my shoulder, raised my right hand and played an air violin.

He got closer to the window. I pointed to the doors to my right again and to my mouth and to him. *Talk.*

He pointed to his wrist. *Do you know what time it is?*

I shrugged. *So what?* I played the violin again.

He nodded. But didn't move.

I hinted at the violin, applauded, put my hand over my heart. *It was great.*

He nodded. And stood staring at me. I was giving up hope, when he pointed to his right, my left. He wanted us to go the other way.

We walked side by side. We turned the corner—of

the sidewalk for me, of the counters for him. He was heading for a door. He indicated to me to keep walking beyond the end of the windows. I arrived in front of an exterior glass door, the bottom half of which was glazed. When Morton hit a light switch, I could see it gave onto a corridor. He came up to the door.

He looked me up and down, warily.

I wet my fingertip and wrote "Rankin" backwards and in reverse on the door.

He nodded. And wrote a question mark and pointed at me.

I wrote an exclamation mark and pointed at him.

After eyeing me for another few seconds, he pulled from his pocket a heavily laden key ring. He introduced a key into a keyhole in the wall and turned it a quarter. Then he unlocked the door. It had three deadbolts. The door opened.

"Listen," I said, "I just wanted to tell you that your concerto was fantastic. It blew me away. I didn't expect anything like it. That discordant violin, it was—"

"I can't keep the door open like this. Come on in."

I stepped in quickly. "Thank you. But I don't want to bother you."

"That's all right."

He locked the door behind me and turned the key in the wall back a quarter.

"I've never heard anything like that discordant

violin before. Most beautiful thing I've ever heard in my life."

Morton smiled. He wasn't looking at me.

"Great, great. Thank you. Uh . . . I have to work. We can talk while I'm working."

"Okay."

We walked across the newly polished floor.

"Have you composed much else?"

"Lots of stuff. Here, do you want to clean the phones for me? While we're talking? I'll show you how."

"Sure, I'd be happy to."

He took a cloth and a white plastic bottle from the cart. I followed him behind the counters.

"You do it like this. You squirt the cloth with some of this." It smelt of alcohol. He picked up a phone. "Then you wipe the body, the cradle—you push down on the plunger, you don't try to clean around it—then the buttons. Then you do the handset. Make sure you wipe the mouthpiece. Then you put the handset back, wiping it so there aren't any fingerprints. Okay?"

"Got it."

A bank has a lot of phones. Morton fetched a bottle of Windex and a clean rag. He began to clean the Plexiglas panes between the tellers' booths. It occurred to me: you're in Washington, it's the middle of the night, you're in a bank, you're with Mozart, and you're cleaning phones.

"You should try to get your concerto broadcast by a radio station."

"We're non-professional. A 'recreational orchestra,' as someone told us once."

"Maybe you could get a professional orchestra to play it?"

"That might be an idea."

One that had led them nowhere, I guessed from the tone of his voice.

I finished the phones. "So was Donald Rankin a friend of yours?"

"Yeah, he was."

No details forthcoming. I wasn't doing this right. I had to try another tack.

"Do you want me to do the desks?"

"That would be helpful." He got me another rag, a soft chamois one. "You're just dusting. If you move or lift anything, make sure you put it back exactly where it was, especially papers."

"Yep."

A bank has a lot of desks. He went over to do the other side of the panes. We worked in silence.

"I wish I had finished it," he said, at last. "On our own we can play it no problem. But in public, in front of everyone, I get so nervous. All those damn mistakes. I wanted it to be perfect."

"I think what Fife said was true. It didn't matter."

He said nothing. I returned to my work.

He finished the panes and came over to help me with the desks.

"You know, at least Bach is a part of it all. If he were taken away, some things would collapse. There would be a hole in Germany and a hole in us. Me? What do I do? I'm a recreational product. I'm a tennis ball. I'm a small-time rival of playing cards and crossword puzzles and game shows. Small-time—Christ, not even that. I've been working here for eleven years. I put up a poster in the staff room, with my name underlined. The man who's been cleaning your workplace for eleven years. A world premiere. Did any of them come? Not one. It's all a fucking waste of life. I'll get the vacuum cleaner."

He walked to the floor polisher, pushed down on its handles and rolled it away. He came back with a vacuum cleaner. I was expecting something big and industrial, barrel-shaped, but he brought back a tiny thing on three wheels with a very long cord. He plugged it in. He saw me looking at it.

"Vacuum cleaners are like dogs," he said. "The smaller they are, the louder."

He turned it on. Indeed. This chihuahua of a vacuum cleaner made more noise than an airplane engine.

"YOU MOVE—" Morton shouted. He turned it off. "You move the chairs and wastepaper baskets and I'll vacuum, okay?"

I nodded and he turned it on again. The thing

sucked in a fearsome way. I was surprised it didn't eat the carpet pile right off the burlap. I rolled the chairs about and lifted the wastepaper baskets.

A bank has a lot of carpeting.

Morton started speaking again. He didn't seem to mind having to shout. In fact, I suspect he was glad of the noise.

"I READ IN A MAGAZINE ONCE ABOUT THIS CHO-REOGRAPHER WHO LAUGHED—LAUGHED—ABOUT PEOPLE WHO THOUGHT DANCE WAS JUST ENTER-TAINMENT. HE SAID DANCE WAS A PHILOSOPHY OF LIFE. I LIKE THAT—A PHILOSOPHY OF LIFE. YOU KNOW WHERE I WAS HAPPIEST WITH MY MUSIC? YOU WANT ME TO TELL YOU?"

Yesyesyes, I nodded.

"WAY BACK IN VIETNAM. I WENT OVER WHEN I WAS NINETEEN. I THOUGHT IT WOULD BE AN AD-VENTURE. I GOT THERE IN OCTOBER OF 1967 AND WHERE DO I END UP IN JANUARY? KHE SANH! HAVE YOU HEARD OF KHE SANH? YOU HAVEN'T? IT WAS A SIEGE. ALL THOSE GREAT MODERN WEAPONS, BUT IT WAS LIKE THE MIDDLE AGES. WE WERE SURROUNDED SOLID BY THE NVA. FUCKING WESTMORELAND SAID WE SHOULD STICK IT OUT. THING LASTED SEVENTY-SEVEN DAYS. SEVENTY-SEVEN DAYS SURROUNDED BY PEOPLE WHO EVERY DAY SHOT AT YOU AND LAUNCHED ROCKET AND MORTAR ATTACKS ON YOU. IT WAS HELL. WE BUILT A MAZE OF TRENCHES AND

LIVED IN THEM LIKE WET RATS. THAT'S WHERE I MET DON RANKIN. YOU KNOW WHERE HE WAS FROM? MOSCOW MILLS, MISSOURI. CAN YOU BELIEVE IT? HERE WE WERE FIGHTING THE NVA AND THIS GUY COMES FROM A PLACE CALLED MOSCOW MILLS. WE NEARLY SHOT HIM WHEN HE TOLD US THAT. I STILL LAUGH ABOUT IT NOW. I'VE BEEN THERE, ACTUALLY, TO MOSCOW MILLS."

He paused for a moment, gazing into midair. He started vacuuming again in clean, easy sweeps.

"ANYWAY, I'D WRITE LETTERS HOME AND THERE WERE SO MANY THINGS I WANTED TO SAY. BUT I COULDN'T SAY THEM. I'D GET BOGGED DOWN. MY SENTENCES WERE SO CLOGGED THEY NEEDED A DRAIN. AND I DIDN'T WANT TO SCARE MY PARENTS OR MY SISTER. SO FOR THE HELL OF IT I STARTED WRITING DOWN THE SONGS I HEARD OVER THE RADIO. I'D WRITE DOWN THE LYRICS, TOO, BUT OFTEN I'D CHANGE THEM AND WRITE MY OWN. DO YOU KNOW WHAT ELVIS PRESLEY SOUNDS LIKE ON THE VIOLIN? OR MOTOWN? OR THE MAMAS AND THE PAPAS? I LOVED PLAYING 'MONDAY, MONDAY.'"

He had a big grin.

"I MANAGED TO GET A VIOLIN IN SAIGON. I TOOK MUSIC IN HIGH SCHOOL. I COULD READ AND WRITE IT ALL RIGHT. THANK GOD I HAD THAT VIO-LIN. SO I USED TO WRITE DOWN THESE SONGS WITH MY OWN LYRICS AND SEND THEM TO MY PARENTS

TO TELL THEM THAT I WAS ALIVE AND ALL RIGHT.
THEY CAN'T READ MUSIC, BUT THEY'D READ THE
LYRICS LIKE THEY WERE LETTERS. WHOLE THING
WAS KIND OF DUMB, I SUPPOSE, BUT THAT'S WHAT I
DID. THEN I GOT TIRED OF BUSTING MY HEAD LIS-
TENING TO A RADIO TRYING TO FIGURE OUT THE
KEY AND THE NOTES. I WANTED TO DO SOME-
THING—HOW CAN I PUT IT?"

He flicked the air with his hand.

"SOMETHING MORE REMOVED FROM ALL THIS
SHIT IN VIETNAM, SOMETHING THAT WOULD RE-
TURN MY SANITY TO ME. THAT'S WHEN I STARTED
WRITING MY OWN STUFF. COMBAT TURNED ME
INTO A COMPOSER. I'D LOOK AT THOSE GREEN HILLS
EXPLODING WITH BOMBS AND I'D HEAR SCARLATTI,
BACH, HANDEL, CORELLI. THE BAROQUE MADE SENSE
TO ME IN KHE SANH. WHEN THINGS WERE CALM
AND IT WASN'T RAINING, I'D FIND MYSELF A DRY,
SHADED PLACE AND I'D GET TO WORK. THE GUYS
LOVED IT. I REMEMBER WILBUR WAS PLUCKING MY
VIOLIN ONCE—HE WAS ANOTHER FRIEND—AND HE
SNAPPED A STRING. YOU SHOULD HAVE SEEN HIS
FACE. I MEAN, I HAD EXTRA STRINGS, IT WASN'T A
PROBLEM. BUT HE WAS SO SORRY I THOUGHT HE WAS
GOING TO SHOOT HIMSELF. YOU KNOW WHAT HE
DID? HE WAS A RADIO OPERATOR. I DON'T KNOW
HOW HE MANAGED IT, BUT THE NEXT AIRDROP
DELIVERY HAD ENOUGH STRINGS IN IT TO FIT AN

ENTIRE VIOLIN SECTION. WILBUR ALSO GOT ME
STAFF PAPER. YEAH, THEY LOVED IT. I'D START PLAY-
ING AND IMMEDIATELY, IF THERE WAS A RADIO ON
NEARBY, IT WOULD BE TURNED OFF. THAT'S WHERE I
WAS HAPPIEST WITH MY MUSIC, IN A SHITHOLE IN
HELL IN THE MIDDLE OF A WAR."

We'd finished. He turned the vacuum cleaner off.
The quiet was a relief.

"My life since then has been a waste of time," he
said.

He unplugged the cord.

"You want a drink?"

"No thanks."

He walked over and picked up the Mr. Clean bottle.

"They don't allow it," he said with a smile, a sad sort
of smile. He took a gulp and stood looking into space.
Several seconds went by. He held the Mr. Clean bottle
by the neck, swinging it gently.

"Fuck, I wish we'd played it right."

"You'll play it again some other time, and then
you'll get it right."

He nodded. But he wasn't convinced.

I couldn't get through to him. I would take all the
alcohol, loneliness and wasted time in the world in ex-
change for creating something so beautiful. I suppose
it's easier saying that than living through it, but still. But
still.

"Yeah, Donald Rankin was a friend of mine." He

took a sudden, deep breath, in and out. "I'll put the vacuum cleaner away." He disappeared with it.

"This is a lousy, boring job," he said when he came
back. "It pays the bills and nobody bothers me, that's as
good as it gets. But there's one thing I like. It's the last
thing I do when I'm finished down here. I always
check. Look: one, two, three."

He pointed to three desks.

"It's mostly women who work here."

He pulled open the top left drawer of one of the
desks. It contained what you'd expect from a drawer in
a desk in a bank, the usual assorted stationery.

"There." He nudged forward with his index finger
till I saw what he meant. Tucked in beside the en-
velopes with the bank's logo. Hardly visible.

A tampon.

He went to another desk. Another drawer. "There."
Another tampon.

A third desk. A third drawer. A third tampon.

"There are more women here than that, but the
others don't leave any in their desks. Or maybe they do,
in the locked drawers. Or maybe they keep them in
their purses. I don't know."

He carefully took out the third tampon. Its wrapping paper was worn and wrinkled.

"These things are the only sign of life in this place.
I see one of them and I think, *Blood...sex...children...
love.* I remember once I saw this graffiti on a wall in

Philadelphia: 'I am magical: I can bleed for five days and not die.' I like that. Everything else here is dead. Dead and bloodless. I hate this place. I hate it because whenever I come here during the day I like it and nearly fall for it. It's comfortable and warm, the people are nice, and you know what's expected of you. I say to myself, *You should get a daytime job here. The pay's good, better than what you make now, anyway, you work with people, the hours are sane—hey, why not?* Then I catch myself. This place is dangerous it's so cunning. It crawls up on you stealthily. You get used to it, the routine, you know. You start to think it's normal. Finally you think there's nothing else. Then you blink, forty years have gone by, and your life's over. Sometimes I come here during the day and I look in from the outside and I ask myself, *Why don't these people ask for more?* There used to be a fourth desk. Then about a year ago the tampon disappeared. I thought that was great. I bet it came as a surprise. *Damn period. How annoying,* she must have thought. But when I emptied the wastepaper basket I found the tampon—unused. It had been wrapped in paper and thrown away. I woke up early the next day and got here before the bank closed. At the desk I saw a woman in her early fifties: Laura Brooks."

He pointed to a desk. There was a grey plastic sign with that name written in black letters.

"I didn't speak to her. I just looked at her while pretending to read some pamphlets. She smiled sometimes when people spoke to her, but mostly she had this serious, at-work expression. I felt sad for her. The end of her fertility. A private drama in a public place. I've written something about her. The Laura Brooks Concerto. I name all my pieces after people. It helps me focus. It's a concerto in two movements for flute, violin and orchestra. I'll be finished soon."

He put the tampon back in its exact place, turning and prodding it till he was satisfied.

"Yeah, I'm going to get down to it and finish it."

Morton looked about. He looked at the clock on the wall. It was past one in the morning.

"Uh ... we've finished here. But I still have a ton of offices to clean, back there and upstairs, and you're not really supposed to be here."

"Hey, no problem. I don't mean to be a bother. I should be getting home anyway."

We returned to the corridor where I had come in.

"Here, I'll show you where I always work."

We turned right. He opened the third door on the left and switched the light on. It was a plain, ordinary office: a chair, a desk, two chairs in front of the desk, two filing cabinets, a plant, a pastel-coloured print on the wall of a sailing boat at sea.

"Before cleaning, or during, or after, whenever I feel like it, I come here and I work on my music. I have a stand in my locker. I don't know why I work here. There are bigger and nicer offices. Just habit, I guess."

"Is this where you wrote the Rankin Concerto?"

"No, I wrote the Rankin years ago. But I've written a lot of other stuff here." He paused. "I like this office. I'm happy here."

He turned the light off. We walked to the glass door that gave onto the street.

"I'm glad you liked my concerto. I appreciate that," he said.

"It was extraordinary. I'll never forget it."

"That's great, that's great."

He turned the key in the wall and unlocked the door.

"It was an honour meeting you, Mr. Morton."

"Right. Thanks for helping me clean."

We shook hands.

I was outside. He was holding the door open.

"Next time I come down to Washington I'll check if you're playing again."

"Yeah, you do that. We try to play two, three times a year."

"I'll check for sure."

"Yeah, great, thanks. Bye."

"Bye."

He closed and locked the door and turned the alarm system back on. Before turning away, he smiled and waved at me.

I hurried to the corner and across the street to where his car was. I was in the dark there and he couldn't see me easily. I watched him as he crossed the floor of the bank, took hold of the cart and disappeared to the right.

It was late, close to two-thirty, when I got home. My friend was still up. He was in an expansive mood. His evening had been productive; his desk was a mess of reports read and notes written. It struck me then how many parallel hours there are. There were my hours and there were his hours. He asked me how my concert had been. I didn't know what to say. For some reason, at that moment, I didn't want to mention the name John Morton or his concerto or the discordant violin. I had a sudden urge to cry. I took a deep breath and said my concert had been "very good." My friend replied, "I've never even heard of the Merridew Theater." I asked him about his day. He told me the latest about Eastern.

The first thing I did the next morning was go to the Vietnam Veterans Memorial. It's strangely moving. The earth yields to a great wedge on whose black marble walls the names of the war dead are inscribed. It's a tactile memorial; you can touch the names. In fact, you can't help but touch them. And there he was. I found him. Donald J. Rankin. I touched his name gently. Then I moved away, and I wept over this war that had nothing to do with me and that I know so little about.

THIS WAS SOME MONTHS AGO. It's now the summer of
1989. Williams and his gang may have played again
since I saw them. Perhaps they've played the Laura
Brooks Concerto for Flute, Violin and Orchestra.

For a while I told people about the concert at the
Merridew. But I wasn't pleased with the reactions I got.
At first I spoke of "the composer John Morton." This
drew blank faces, so I expanded: "the American composer John Morton." It still wasn't enough. I could tell
that what was needed was "an American composer
called John Morton." But that irked me. As if you have
to say "an Austrian composer called Wolfgang Mozart"
to be understood. Now I pretty well keep John Morton
to myself.

My friend has moved from Washington, DC. He
still works for Price Waterhouse, but in New York now.
We keep in touch.

Eastern Airlines has gone bankrupt. The affair is
still going on, but I've stopped reading about it. Last I
heard, Peter Ueberroth, the man who organized the
1984 L.A. Olympics, was getting involved.

I've been accepted to law school. I don't want to be
a lawyer, but a law degree is a good springboard, I'm
told. Springboard to what? I'm bright—people tell me
that—but I don't know what I want to do. I'm restless.
I'm afraid that one day I'll be working somewhere—tie,
desk, office, the routine—and I'll look up and I'll see a

man eyeing me from the outside and I'll know from his expression that he's thinking, *Why doesn't he ask for more?*

I'm afraid that late one evening, perhaps after relating an unlikely anecdote about a musical janitor, I'll jump to my feet, upsetting the chair, and I'll hear myself shout, "Do you hear? I had it all there; so; within reach of my hand."

Manners
of
Dying

Manner of Dying 18

Dear Mrs. Barlow,

As warden of Cantos Correctional Institution and pursuant to the Freedom of Information Act, I am writing to inform you of how your son Kevin Barlow faced up to his execution by hanging for the crimes for which he was convicted.

For his last supper, Kevin ordered: vegetable soup with crackers; turkey (white meat only) with gravy; peas, carrots and potatoes; a salad with a Caesar dressing; red wine; cheesecake. He did not touch his meal.

Kevin did not avail himself of Father Preston's services.

Periodic checks throughout the evening and night indicated that Kevin was agitated and did not sleep at all. He was seen pacing about his cell; sitting on his bed; and holding himself up to the window by his fingers and looking out.

At 6:00 a.m., when Father Preston's services were offered again, Kevin asked to see him. What transpired between them is protected by the code of ethics concerning confidentiality and is known only by Father Preston and the Almighty.

At 6:50 a.m., when I entered Kevin's cell with the attending personnel, I found Kevin standing on the far side of the cell, beneath the window, with Father Preston at his side. I would describe your son as: pale and frightened. I read him the judgment ordering his execution as handed down by the legal and legitimate courts of the land in accordance with the law, informed him that I was here to carry out this sentence, and asked him if he understood this. Kevin did not react, but I believe he understood. I asked him to accompany me. Because of his trembling, he seemed incapable of walking, and two guards assisted him. There was no violence, I assure you.

As we walked down the corridor, Kevin had difficulty staying on his feet and required the continued assistance of the guards. His breathing was laboured. When he caught sight of the gallows, it became more laboured.

Doctor Lowe assured Kevin that the execution would be painless, which it is. Kevin grabbed hold of the doctor's arm and asked him in a quavering voice how he knew this. Doctor Lowe explained that, in hanging, death is brought on not by strangulation but by the snapping of the neck, which is quick and leads to an instant loss of consciousness, so there is no time for pain. Doctor Lowe firmly assured Kevin that he would feel no physical pain.

Kevin's medical file indicated that he was a smoker, so I offered him a last cigarette. He took it in his hand, but did not bring it to his mouth. I told him he had a minute to collect and compose himself, and offered him a chair. He sat down and stared at the ground.

After the minute, I asked Kevin if he had any last words or any last message he wished to have transmitted. Short of breath, he said: "Tell my mother I love her." I assured him that I would tell you. He tried to speak again, but he was overcome with such a stutter that despite my best efforts I could not understand him.

I shook hands with Kevin and wished him farewell.

Mister Rothway and the guards conveyed Kevin to the gallows and made him stand straight over the trap. Mister Rothway tied his hands behind his back, covered his head with a hood and put the noose around his neck. Kevin relieved himself in his pants.

At 7:01 a.m., the trap was released and your son Kevin Barlow died painlessly.

Please believe that I share in your grief.

Yours truly,

Harry Parlington
Warden,
Cantos Correctional Institution

HP:ym

Dear Mrs. Barlow,

As warden of Cantos Correctional Institution and pursuant to the Freedom of Information Act, I am writing to inform you of how your son Kevin Barlow faced up to his execution by hanging for the crimes for which he was convicted.

For his last supper, Kevin ordered: boiled potatoes. He ate only one potato, but he asked that the plate be left for the night.

Father Preston stayed with Kevin for twenty-one minutes. What transpired between them is protected by the code of ethics concerning confidentiality and is known only by Father Preston and the Almighty.

Periodic checks throughout the evening and night indicated that Kevin was calm. He was seen pacing about his cell, and holding himself up to the window

by his fingers and looking out. At approximately 1
a.m., he lay down on his bed, covered himself with his
blanket and apparently fell asleep.

At 6:00 a.m., when Father Preston's services were
offered again, Kevin did not respond.

At 6:50 a.m., when I entered Kevin's cell with the
attending personnel, I found Kevin lying on his bed,
covered with his blanket, unconscious. Doctor Lowe
examined him immediately and declared him dead.

Kevin took his own life. The autopsy confirmed
that he died of asphyxiation caused by forcing down
his throat a potato dropped into one of his socks. The
estimated time of death was between 1 a.m. and 3 a.m.

This is not the way I would have had it (none of
this is the way I would have had it), but that Kevin
chose to do this, on his own terms and in his own
time, can perhaps be a comfort to you.

Please believe that I share in your grief.

Yours truly,

Harry Parlington
Warden,
Cantos Correctional Institution

HP:ym

Dear Mrs. Barlow,

As warden of Cantos Correctional Institution and pursuant to the Freedom of Information Act, I am writing to inform you of how your son Kevin Barlow faced up to his execution by hanging for the crimes for which he was convicted.

For his last supper, Kevin ordered: half an avocado with a Thousand Island dressing; salmon with a lemon-butter sauce; carrots and potatoes; Australian white wine; chocolate ice cream. He did not touch his meal, except for the ice cream, of which he asked for seconds.

Father Preston stayed with Kevin for sixteen minutes. What transpired between them is protected by the code of ethics concerning confidentiality and is known only by Father Preston and the Almighty.

Periodic checks throughout the evening and night indicated that Kevin was very agitated and did not sleep at all. He was seen pacing about his cell frantically; muttering to himself; and holding himself up to the window by his fingers and looking out.

At 6:00 a.m., when Father Preston's services were offered again, Kevin did not respond beyond a burst of laughter and some muttering.

At 6:50 a.m., when I entered Kevin's cell with the attending personnel, I found Kevin sitting on his bed, apparently in a state of mirth; he was chuckling. In fact, at the sight of me, he began to laugh. I would describe your son as: flushed and agitated. In spite of his continued laughing, I read him the judgment ordering his execution as handed down by the legal and legitimate courts of the land in accordance with the law, informed him that I was here to carry out this sentence, and asked him if he understood this. Kevin only laughed. I became concerned for his sanity. I asked Doctor Lowe if he could be considered legally insane, and if, therefore, the legality of his execution could be put into doubt. Doctor Lowe told me it was his professional opinion that Kevin's laughter was due to psychological stress, not insanity, and that Kevin understood the situation. I asked Kevin to accompany me. He continued to laugh and did not move. He offered a bit of resistance to the guards—no more than pulling his arms away and turning—but then he complied. There was no violence, I assure you.

As we walked down the corridor, Kevin kept laughing, and he had difficulty staying on his feet and required the continued assistance of the guards. When he caught sight of the gallows, he laughed even harder. I became concerned in view of the extreme redness of his face and his painful gasps for breath. Doctor Lowe told me there was nothing that could be done at this stage, and that it was not dangerous, the worst that could happen being a fainting spell due to lack of oxygen.

Doctor Lowe assured Kevin that the execution would be painless, which it is, but I'm not sure he heard.

Kevin's medical file indicated that he was a smoker, so I offered him a last cigarette. He kept laughing and ignored me. I told him he had a minute to collect and compose himself, and offered him a chair. He fell on the chair and continued laughing.

After the minute, I asked Kevin if he had any last words or any last message he wished to have transmitted. He did not seem to hear me. I insisted, trying to make myself understood above the roar of his laughter, to no avail.

I attempted to shake hands with Kevin, but he repeatedly hid his hand as if we were playing a game, saying "Whoops!" each time. I wished him farewell.

Mister Rothway and the guards conveyed Kevin to the gallows and made him stand straight over the trap. Mister Rothway tied his hands behind his back, covered his head with a hood and put the noose around his neck. To the very end, Kevin did not stop laughing.

At 6:58 a.m., the trap was released and your son Kevin Barlow died painlessly.

Please believe that I share in your grief.

Yours truly,

Harry Parlington
Warden,
Cantos Correctional Institution

HP:ym

Manner of Dying 534

Dear Mrs. Barlow,

As warden of Cantos Correctional Institution and pursuant to the Freedom of Information Act, I am writing to inform you of how your son Kevin Barlow faced up to his execution by hanging for the crimes for which he was convicted.

For his last supper, Kevin ordered: caviar; champagne; cigarillos. Though an unusual request, we obliged. He gobbled down the caviar and drank his champagne in a single draft. He asked for more champagne. I authorized another half-bottle. When it disappeared as fast as the first and he asked for a third, I said no. There are limits.

Kevin bluntly did not avail himself of Father Preston's services.

Periodic checks throughout the evening and night

indicated that Kevin was agitated and did not sleep at all. He was seen sitting on his bed, smoking cigarillo after cigarillo; pacing about his cell; and holding himself up to the window by his fingers and looking out. At 10:11 p.m., I was informed that he wanted to see me. I could hear him hollering from a hundred yards away. When I arrived at his cell, he asked me why we were wasting his time and why he couldn't be hanged right away. I explained to him that there was a set legal procedure that had to be followed. I ascribed his bravado to nervous tension and gave him another box of cigarillos.

At 6:00 a.m., when Father Preston's services were offered again, Kevin replied that he'd prefer a topless waitress with a full tray of drinks, and he began to holler for me again.

At 6:12 a.m., when I arrived early with the attending personnel, I found Kevin kicking at his cell door, shouting for things to move. When the door was opened, he bounded out and had to be restrained by the guards, though with minimal violence, I assure you. I would describe your son as: flushed, angry and impatient. I began to read him the judgment ordering his execution as handed down by the legal and legitimate courts of the land in accordance with the law, but he kept interrupting. I quickly finished, informed him that I was here to carry out this sentence, and asked him if he understood this. Before

I had even finished, he was shouting:"Yesyesyesyesyes!" and was pushing us out the cell. I dispensed with asking him to accompany me.

In spite of the guards' efforts, we raced rather than walked down the corridor. When Kevin caught sight of the gallows, he charged so that he was halfway up the steps before Doctor Lowe could assure him that the execution would be painless, which it is. Kevin replied: "But is it fast?" The guards brought him back down.

I offered Kevin a last cigarillo. He refused it. I told him he had a minute to collect and compose himself, and offered him a chair. He refused angrily.

I did not insist and asked him if he had any last words or any last message he wished to have transmitted. He said: "Stop wasting my time!"

I shook hands with Kevin and wished him farewell. He shook my hand impatiently, and those of Doctor Lowe, Father Preston and Mister Rothway, wishing us all speedy promotions.

Kevin pushed and made another break for it and got to the top of the gallows before Mister Rothway or the guards. He put the noose around his neck and started kicking at the trap. Mister Rothway tied his hands behind his back and covered his head with a hood.

At 6:16 a.m., the trap was released and your son Kevin Barlow died painlessly.

Please believe that I share in your grief.

Yours truly,

Harry Parlington
Warden,
Cantos Correctional Institution

HP:ym

Dear Mrs. Barlow,

As warden of Cantos Correctional Institution and pursuant to the Freedom of Information Act, I am writing to inform you of how your son Kevin Barlow faced up to his execution by hanging for the crimes for which he was convicted.

For his last supper, Kevin ordered: a salad with a blue cheese dressing; two cheeseburgers (extra old Cheddar cheese) all-dressed; french fries; sparkling mineral water; apple pie with vanilla ice cream. He ate everything except for the hamburger patties, which he removed and wrapped in a napkin and left on his plate, and he asked for more mineral water.

Father Preston stayed with Kevin for one hour and twenty-two minutes. What transpired between them is protected by the code of ethics concerning confidentiality and is known only by Father Preston and the Almighty.

Periodic checks throughout the evening and night indicated that Kevin was very agitated and did not sleep at all. He was seen pacing about his cell frantically, and holding himself up to the window by his fingers and looking out.

At 6:00 a.m., when Father Preston's services were offered again, Kevin asked to see him. As the door was opened, Kevin made an attempt to get away. In the scuffle, Father Preston was hit in the face. The guards pushed Kevin back into the cell and closed the door. Kevin insisted that he still wanted to see Father Preston. Father Preston was willing. I was informed of what had happened. I deemed that Kevin was not acting in good faith, and instructed that if he wanted to speak with Father Preston he would have to do so through the barred opening of the door. There are limits. Kevin and Father Preston spoke for three minutes. What transpired between them is protected by the code of ethics concerning confidentiality and is known only by Father Preston and the Almighty.

At 6:50 a.m., when I entered Kevin's cell with the attending personnel, we found that Kevin had attempted to block the door by jamming his blanket between it and the floor. Kevin was standing on the far side of the cell, beneath the window, shouting at us to leave him alone.

I would describe your son as: pale, frightened and very aggressive. In spite of his continued shouting, I read him the judgment ordering his execution as handed down by the legal and legitimate courts of the land in accordance with the law, informed him that I was here to carry out this sentence, and asked him if he understood this. He shouted that he didn't. I repeated myself. When he still claimed not to understand, I deemed that Kevin was not acting in good faith, and asked him to accompany me. He refused. Sadly I must inform you that a violent struggle ensued, though the guards used no more force than was strictly needed to restrain Kevin, I assure you.

As Kevin was carried down the corridor, bound and gagged, he continued to struggle. When he caught sight of the gallows, he struggled even harder.

Doctor Lowe assured Kevin that the execution would be painless, which it is, but I'm not sure he heard.

Kevin's medical file indicated that he was a smoker, but I dispensed with offering him a last cigarette. I told him he had a minute to collect and compose himself, but I dispensed with offering him a chair. His struggling was such that the guards had to keep him on the floor to contain him.

After the minute, I asked Kevin if he had any last words or any last message he wished to have transmitted, and I removed his gag. He roared abuse.

I wished Kevin farewell, but I could not shake his hand because his hands were tied.

Mister Rothway and the guards carried Kevin to the gallows and held him straight over the trap. Mister Rothway forced a hood over his head and put the noose around his neck. To the very end, Kevin did not stop shouting and struggling.

At 7:04 a.m., the trap was released and your son Kevin Barlow died painlessly.

Please believe that I share in your grief.

Yours truly,

Harry Parlington
Warden,
Cantos Correctional Institution

HP:ym

Manner of Dying 760

Dear Mrs. Barlow,

As warden of Cantos Correctional Institution and pursuant to the Freedom of Information Act, I am writing to inform you of how your son Kevin Barlow faced up to his execution by hanging for the crimes for which he was convicted.

For his last supper, Kevin ordered: a pear. He did not eat it.

Kevin did not avail himself of Father Preston's services. Instead, he asked for pen and paper. He was given a ballpoint pen and fifty sheets of lined paper.

Periodic checks throughout the evening and night indicated that Kevin was calm. He was seen pacing about his cell; holding himself up to the window by his fingers and looking out; and sitting on the floor, writing, using his bed as a desk. At 1:14 a.m., he asked for more paper. He was given an extra hundred sheets.

At 6:00 a.m., when Father Preston's services were offered again, Kevin once again said no.

At 6:50 a.m., when I entered Kevin's cell with the attending personnel, I found Kevin sitting on the floor, writing, using his bed as a desk. I would describe your son as: pale, busy and flustered. Before I had even said a word, he pleaded to be given a little more time to finish what he was writing. To his left was an amazing pile of papers, each densely covered in handwriting. I asked him how much more time he wanted. He replied: "Not long. Three more pages." In matters like this, I have some discretionary power. I told Kevin to call out when he was finished but to be quick. We left the cell, the door was closed and he was left alone.

At 7:18 a.m., Kevin called out. When I entered his cell with the attending personnel, I found him holding himself up to the window by his fingers and looking out. The papers on his bed were neatly stacked. I would describe your son as: pale and calm. He thanked me for the extra time and asked for a large envelope. I sent a guard to get one. I read Kevin the judgment ordering his execution as handed down by the legal and legitimate courts of the land in accordance with the law, informed him that I was here to carry out this sentence, and asked him if he understood this. Kevin replied that he did. I asked him to accompany me. Clutching his papers and the envelope, he walked out with me.

As we walked down the corridor, I slightly ahead of him and the others several feet behind, Kevin put the papers in the large envelope and sealed it. When he caught sight of the gallows, he groaned and became frightened, but he squeezed the envelope in his arms and this seemed to comfort him.

Doctor Lowe assured Kevin that the execution would be painless, which it is. Kevin nodded.

Kevin's medical file indicated that he was a smoker, so I offered him a last cigarette. He shook his head. I told him he had a minute to collect and compose himself, and offered him a chair. He sat down and stared at the envelope in his hands.

After the minute, I asked Kevin if he had any last words or any last message he wished to have transmitted. Short of breath, he said: "Tell my mother I love her and she mustn't be sad. Tell her here I am." And he handed me the envelope, which I enclose with this letter. I assured him that I would tell you and that you would receive the envelope.

I shook hands with Kevin and wished him farewell.

Kevin walked up to the gallows with Mister Rothway and the guards and stood over the trap. At this time, he said: "It *is* a beautiful world, isn't it?" I agreed with him that it is. Mister Rothway tied his hands behind his back, covered his head with a hood and put the noose around his neck.

At 7:29 a.m., the trap was released and your son Kevin Barlow died painlessly.

Please believe that I share in your grief.

Yours truly,

Harry Parlington
Warden,
Cantos Correctional Institution

enc.
HP:ym

Manner of Dying 985

Dear Mrs. Barlow,

As warden of Cantos Correctional Institution and pursuant to the Freedom of Information Act, I am writing to inform you of how your son Kevin Barlow faced up to his execution by hanging for the crimes for which he was convicted.

For his last supper, Kevin ordered: two grilled hot dogs, all-dressed; french fries; root beer. He ate everything except for the hot-dog wieners, which he removed and wrapped in a napkin and left on his plate, and he asked for more root beer.

Father Preston stayed with Kevin for fifty-five minutes. What transpired between them is protected by the code of ethics concerning confidentiality and is known only by Father Preston and the Almighty.

Periodic checks throughout the evening and night

indicated that Kevin was agitated and did not sleep at
all. He was seen pacing about his cell; sitting on his
bed; and holding himself up to the window by his
fingers and looking out. At 2:36 a.m., I was informed
that he wanted to see me. When I arrived at his cell,
he asked me if he could go outside. In matters like
this, I have some discretionary power. Cantos has a
secure interior courtyard. I instructed the guards to
escort him to it and to let him do as he pleased, within
reason. Kevin spent the whole night stretching; doing
push-ups, sit-ups and other calisthenics; skipping on
the spot and bobbing his head from side to side;
jogging, both forwards and backwards; shadowboxing;
and lying on the ground looking up at the sky. It was a
clear night. The stars were countless.

At 6:00 a.m., when Father Preston's services were
offered again, Kevin asked to see him. What
transpired between them is protected by the code of
ethics concerning confidentiality and is known only
by Father Preston and the Almighty.

At 6:50 a.m., when I entered the courtyard with
the attending personnel, I found Kevin and Father
Preston walking side by side. I would describe your
son as: pale and agitated. I read him the judgment
ordering his execution as handed down by the legal
and legitimate courts of the land in accordance with
the law, informed him that I was here to carry out this
sentence, and asked him if he understood this. Kevin

nodded. I asked him to accompany me. He walked out of the courtyard with me.

As we walked down the corridor, I slightly ahead of him and the others several feet behind, Kevin shadowboxed. When he caught sight of the gallows, he went into a frenzy of jabs, hooks and uppercuts.

Doctor Lowe assured Kevin that the execution would be painless, which it is. Kevin nodded.

Kevin's medical file indicated that he was a smoker, so I offered him a last cigarette. He shook his head. I told him he had a minute to collect and compose himself, and offered him a chair. He nodded, but stayed on his feet and continued to shadowbox.

After the minute, I asked Kevin if he had any last words or any last message he wished to have transmitted. Short of breath, he said: "Knockout. First round."

I shook hands with Kevin and wished him farewell.

Kevin slowly jogged up to the gallows with Mister Rothway and the guards and stood over the trap. Mister Rothway tied his hands behind his back, covered his head with a hood and put the noose around his neck. Kevin jogged on the spot and began to hyperventilate loudly.

At 7:00 a.m., the trap was released and your son Kevin Barlow died painlessly.

Please believe that I share in your grief.

Yours truly,

Harry Parlington
Warden,
Cantos Correctional Institution

HP:ym

Manner of Dying 991

Dear Mrs. Barlow,

As warden of Cantos Correctional Institution and pursuant to the Freedom of Information Act, I am writing to inform you of how your son Kevin Barlow faced up to his execution by hanging for the crimes for which he was convicted.

For his last supper, Kevin ordered: a T-bone steak; green beans and potatoes; beer; pistachio ice cream. He did not touch his meal, except for the ice cream.

Kevin did not avail himself of Father Preston's services.

Periodic checks throughout the evening and night indicated that Kevin was agitated and did not sleep at all. He was seen pacing about his cell; sitting on his bed; and holding himself up to the window by his fingers and looking out. At 10:24 p.m., he asked for some magazines. He was given a range of sports, nature and political magazines. At 11:03 p.m., I was informed that he wanted to see me. When I arrived at his cell, he asked me if I wanted to play backgammon. I don't particularly like games, but I agreed. I sent a guard to get a game. Kevin and I spent the whole night playing backgammon. We also talked, he to me for the most part. I asked him if he wanted to have our conversation taped, as a final gift to you. He agreed. A tape recorder was brought into the cell. I enclose the four tapes with this letter. Kevin beat me handily at backgammon.

At 6:00 a.m., when Father Preston's services were offered again, Kevin once again said no. I asked him if he wanted to stop playing. He wanted to continue.

At 6:52 a.m., upon finishing a game, I told Kevin that it was time. He nodded. The door of the cell was opened and the attending personnel entered. I read Kevin the judgment ordering his execution as handed down by the legal and legitimate courts of the land in accordance with the law, informed him that I was here to carry out this sentence, and asked him if he understood this. He nodded. I asked him to accompany me. Clutching the backgammon board, he walked out with me. One of the guards attempted to retrieve the board, but Kevin resisted and I told the guard to let him keep it. There was no violence, I assure you.

As we walked down the corridor, Kevin had difficulty staying on his feet and required the continued assistance of the guards. His breathing was laboured. When he caught sight of the gallows, he groaned and became frightened.

Doctor Lowe assured Kevin that the execution would be painless, which it is. Kevin nodded.

Kevin's medical file indicated that he was a smoker, so I offered him a last cigarette. He shook his head. I told him he had a minute to collect and compose himself, and offered him a chair. He sat down and stared at the ground. At this time, short of breath and with difficulty, he said: "I'm really sorry about all this." I said that I was too.

After the minute, I asked Kevin if he had any last words or any last message he wished to have transmitted. He repeated: "I'm really sorry about all this." I said a second time that I was too. He tried to speak again, but he was overcome with such a stutter that despite my best efforts I could not understand him.

I attempted to shake hands with Kevin, but he would not let go of the backgammon board. I wished him farewell.

Mister Rothway and the guards conveyed Kevin to the gallows and made him stand straight over the trap. Mister Rothway tied a rope around his chest, securing his hands and the backgammon board, covered his head with a hood and put the noose around his neck. Kevin relieved himself in his pants.

At 7:03 a.m., the trap was released and your son Kevin Barlow died painlessly.

Please believe that I share in your grief.

Yours truly,

Harry Parlington
Warden,
Cantos Correctional Institution

enc.
HP:ym

Manner of Dying 1096

Dear Mrs. Barlow,

As warden of Cantos Correctional Institution and pursuant to the Freedom of Information Act, I am writing to inform you of how your son Kevin Barlow faced up to his execution by hanging for the crimes for which he was convicted.

For his last supper, Kevin did not order anything. I came round to tell him that he could have practically anything he wanted, but he said he was not hungry. I told him that if he changed his mind, he should tell the guards.

Father Preston stayed with Kevin all evening and all night. What transpired between them is protected by the code of ethics concerning confidentiality and is known only by Father Preston and the Almighty.

Periodic checks throughout the evening and night

indicated that Kevin was agitated and did not sleep at all. He was seen pacing about his cell; sitting on his bed; holding himself up to the window by his fingers and looking out; and kneeling on the floor with his head on Father Preston's lap. He was heard sobbing.

At 6:50 a.m., when I entered Kevin's cell with the attending personnel, I found Kevin sitting on the floor on the far side of the cell, beneath the window, and Father Preston sitting on the bed. At the sight of me, Kevin began to weep. I would describe your son as: pale and very frightened. I read him the judgment ordering his execution as handed down by the legal and legitimate courts of the land in accordance with the law, informed him that I was here to carry out this sentence, and asked him if he understood this. Kevin only wept, but I believe he understood. I asked him to accompany me. He continued to weep and did not move. As soon as the guards got close, he began to sob loudly and to beg for mercy. He begged repeatedly. I explained to him that sadly it was beyond my power to do anything. Kevin offered a bit of resistance to the guards—no more than pulling his arms away and turning—but there was no violence, I assure you. Because of his trembling, he seemed incapable of walking, and two guards assisted him.

As Kevin was carried down the corridor, he continued to sob and to beg. When he caught sight of the gallows, he relieved himself in his pants and began to thrash about. Suddenly he clutched his left shoulder, whimpered, "I don't feel well," and collapsed. Doctor Lowe examined him immediately and diagnosed cardiac arrest. In spite of several minutes of cardiopulmonary resuscitation, Doctor Lowe could not revive Kevin, and, at 7:06 a.m., he declared him dead. I remember that while Kevin's body was motionless and the doctor and the guards busied themselves, Kevin's eyes stayed on me the whole time.

This is not the way I would have had it. None of this is the way I would have had it.

Please believe that I share in your grief.

Yours truly,

Harry Parlington
Warden,
Cantos Correctional Institution

HP:ym

The
Vita Æterna
Mirror
Company

Mirrors to Last till Kingdom Come

I REMEMBER how I met
my husband. My dear,
sweet husband. It was
the summer of 1928.
I was sixteen and I was
dressed in white. I was also
wearing a straw hat, only
it was too small and
I was always losing it
in the wind. This was
in Grande-Rivière.
I was staying with
Father Bouillon for a
few weeks during the
summer. I was
standing on the veranda,
considering whether

I should go for a walk
with this too-small hat
and always have to keep
my hand on my head to
hold it down, or fetch
another hat that fit me
perfectly but didn't go
as well with my dress.
I was standing on the
veranda, thinking about
it, when a car with two
men stalled just in front
of the house, maybe fifty
feet away. The driver,
a doctor, got out.
I knew he was a doctor
because his car had the
special licence plate that
doctors had in those days.
He opened the hood, leaned
in and did I don't know
what. He seemed in a
hurry. The other man
didn't help; he just sat
in the car, listless.
I found out later that my
future husband was
driving him to the

hospital. He fiddled
about with the engine
for a minute or two and
then fetched the crank.
He turned the crank
and the engine started
up. He hurried back into
the car. I watched this
scene without moving or
saying a word. He didn't
see me, the doctor. The
other man did. The car
disappeared down the
road and then the wind
blew my hat away. I
blah-blah-blah-blah-
blah-blah-blah-blah-
blah-blah-blah-blah-
blah-blah-blah-blah-
blah-blah-blah-blah-
blah-blah-blah-blah-
blah-blah-blah-blah-
blah-blah-blah-blah-
blah-blah-blah-blah-
blah-blah-blah-blah-
blah-blah-blah-blah-
blah-blah-blah-blah-
blah-blah-blah-blah-

Man, she can go on.

blah-blah-blah-blah-
blah-blah-blah-blah-   And always the same
blah-blah-blah-blah-   stories.
blah-blah-blah-blah-
blah-blah-blah-blah-
blah-blah-blah-blah-
blah-blah-blah-blah-   My head will explode
blah-blah-blah-blah-   soon.
blah-blah-blah-blah-
blah-blah-blah-blah-
blah-blah-blah-blah-

(Meanwhile, the machine was chugging away indus-
triously. I put my hand on it. I could feel vibrations.)

blah-blah-blah-blah-
next day, a bright sunny
day, I was walking back
home from the post office
when I saw the very
same car coming towards
me. The sun was behind
me, in the doctor's eyes.
His car didn't have
visors, so he was wearing
a long cap. As the car
came closer, I could see
something written on

it. SEARCHING FOR
A BRIDE, it said in
bright red letters. He
was a bachelor, of course.
He told me later that the
cap was a gift from a
friend. And so, squinting
at the road ahead, as if
actually searching for a
bride at that very
moment, he drove by.
Without seeing me, once
again. He was so
charmingly distracted
sometimes. Once he
blah-blah-blah-blah-
blah-blah-blah-blah-
blah-blah-blah-blah-
blah-blah-blah-blah-
blah-blah-blah-blah-

(I was visiting my grandmother and I had found this
machine in the basement. It looked at first like nothing more than a wooden box.)

blah-blah-blah-blah-
blah-blah-blah-blah-
blah-blah-blah-blah-

blah-blah-blah-blah-
blah-blah-blah-blah-

(More junk, more debris, I thought.)

blah-blah-blah-blah-
blah-blah-blah-blah-
blah-blah-blah-blah-

(My grandmother, you see, clings to her possessions. She throws away nothing. Everything has value. As a young wife she lived through the Great Depression, and shortly after the war her husband died, leaving her alone to raise four children. She suffered through loss, loneliness, poverty, tough times. By dint of hard work, multiple jobs, careful investments and frugality, she managed to raise her children—with great success, in fact: she produced a journalist, a physician, a diplomat poet and a cloistered Benedictine nun. But she can't forget the price of every success along her difficult road. Having known the word "want" for too long, she cannot understand its antonym, "enough." She's like that gold prospector in the Jack London tale who, months after being rescued from starvation, still hoards nuts, biscuits, tinned food and dried fish in his pockets and in every nook and cranny of his room.)

blah-blah-blah-blah-

blah-blah-blah-blah-
carrying a tray with
cups and cookies.
And who should I see
standing squarely in
the living room—I can
still see him perfectly!
Standing so straight.
Looking out with his
kind face and beautiful
eyes. It was Doctor
"Searching for a Bride."
He smiled at me and
I at him. Father Bouillon
had invited the new
doctor in town, telling
him his house was full
of pretty girls. We spoke
a little that day, the
doctor and I, and some
more in the next two
weeks each time he came
by. He was so earnest
and attentive. Later he
told me that on that very
first day, as he was
leaving, he whispered to
Father Bouillon, "There's

my wife." I thought he
blah-blah-blah-blah-
blah-blah-blah-blah-

(I made to push the box aside. It wasn't what I was looking for. I was looking for my grandmother's snowshoe moccasins. I was on all fours in the basement, buried in the cold closet where she keeps her coats. She wanted to go snowshoeing. But the box was unexpectedly heavy, a good fifteen pounds. And it was attractively made of burnished walnut wood.)

blah-blah-blah-blah-
blah-blah-blah-blah-
blah-blah-blah-blah-

(I was curious, so I pulled the box out. It was about fifteen inches wide, twelve inches deep and eight inches high. And it was not a box: it did not open. It was rather some sort of mechanical device. A half-inch slit ran the length of one of the long sides, near the bottom. It had lips of red velvet that revealed, when pulled back, a series of ten or so rollers. Clearly, some thing, some product, came in or out this way. Above this slit, towards the left and embedded in the wood, was a thermometer-like tube with two gradations marked in red, MAX near the top and MIN near the bottom. On the side of the device opposite these two features was a door with a tiny brass doorknob that opened horizontally. The words HIGH-GRADE WHITE SAND ONLY were inscribed on this door, and it opened with a click. It had rounded panels on each side. On one of these I could read the sentence DO NOT FILL OVER THIS LINE. I peered into the cavity that the open door revealed, but could see nothing. I closed the door. On the machine's top side were three holes and a plaque: a small hole near the edge, level with the thermometer-like tube, with the words HIGH-GRADE LIQUID SILVER ONLY inscribed around it; another hole in the opposite corner, this one surrounded by the words HIGH-GRADE OIL ONLY; and, finally, a third, larger, cork-stopped hole midway along one of the sides. The oblong plaque, neatly affixed with golden nails, was in the centre. THE VITA ÆTERNA MIRROR COMPANY, PORT HOPE, ONTARIO, it said. MIRRORS TO LAST TILL KINGDOM COME.)

blah-blah-blah-blah-
blah-blah-blah-blah-
blah-blah-blah-blah-
blah-blah-blah-blah-

("Have you found them? Must I come down?" came a voice of vexed curiosity from above.

"Not yet. A minute more," I replied. I entered the

closet again. Among quantities of shoes, boots, slippers and sneakers, I found the snowshoe moccasins.
And near where the machine had been, I came upon
a grey felt bag with the Vita Æterna Mirror Company
logo on it. I brought it out. Replacing disturbed
footwear and displaced coat hangers with the care of
an archaeologist, I closed the closet door, gathered
up the results of my dig and made my way upstairs.)

blah-blah-blah-blah-
blah-blah-blah-blah-
blah-blah-blah-blah-
blah-blah-blah-blah-
blah-blah-blah-blah-

(She was waiting for me at the top of the stairs. She
is a woman in her early eighties. Vain in a dignified
way, she dresses well, invariably in one shade or
another of purple, her favourite colour. Except for a
few of the normal indignities of old age—cataracts
(operated on), some arthritis, a certain physical sag-
ging—she is in perfect health. Because she saves up
all the conversation she can't have when she's alone
and lonely, she talks nonstop. She listens, but sometimes not really; sometimes one's words are like a
menu from which she'll choose a word or phrase that
will set her off. Her beliefs are solid and well constructed, nearly impregnable, and her ways, though

not intolerant, are nonetheless fixed. Great Questions do not disturb her anymore; her questions now are well within the limits of the Great Answers that have brought her comfort throughout her life. She loves me, for sure, but with the bias of her age. My lack of religiousness saddens her, and my existential hesitations (as exemplified by the fact that I'm considerably closer to thirty than to twenty yet have never held down a real, steady job, bungled my university studies, have accomplished precious little in my life) make her impatient because she can't understand them. She thinks I'm lost. We are meant to stand firm like a house, she tells me, not to be tossed about like a ship. To her, the world is a place run by God where goodness and hard work are ultimately rewarded and evil and sloth are ultimately punished. She is a poor loser at cards—worse than I—and she cheats. My grandmother loves me and I love my grandmother—which doesn't mean that we always get along.)

blah-blah-blah-blah-
blah-blah-blah-blah-
blah-blah-blah-blah-
blah-blah-blah-blah-

("What's this?" she asked.

  "That was my question," I said.

"Oh my," she exclaimed when she had a closer look. Her voice changed. "That old thing. I'd forgotten we still had it." She ran her fingers along it.)

blah-blah-blah-blah-
blah-blah-blah-blah-
blah-blah-blah-blah-
blah-blah-blah-blah-

(I looked about her lair. I will just mention that my grandmother's house is cluttered with furniture that clashes in style; that she owns no complete set of dishware or kitchenware or bedsheets or towels, only the surviving veterans of six decades of housekeeping; that she is well supplied in religious paraphernalia (the crucifix over the front door, the lithographs of the Virgin Mary and of Jesus on the walls, the tourist-shop foreign icons resting on the mantelpiece, the rosary of large wooden beads hanging from the back of a door, the framed colour photos of the Pope, etc.); that after her children moved out she embarked on organized travels from which she brought home the bric-a-brac of the world (an ouzo-bottle lamp, pseudo-antique Greek vases, Easter Island–like sculptures, African masks, a Swiss cuckoo clock, a huge Pacific shell, a Tunisian birdcage, purple Russian dolls, Chinese china, etc.); that she likes fishing and gardening and owns all one might need to pursue those activities—

and there is much, much more. Cubic metres. An ample etcetera of goods, chattels and knick-knacks. My grandmother has a sort of Midas touch: every object she touches becomes eternal. And did I mention that her house is tiny and she owns a piano?)

blah-blah-blah-blah-
blah-blah-blah-blah-
blah-blah-blah-blah-

(I brought the machine to the kitchen table and set the moccasins on the floor.

"So what is it?" I asked.

"It's an old appliance. It's a mirror machine."

As she said this, she nodded towards the living room, at the large mirror above the fireplace. I looked at it.)

blah-blah-blah-blah-
blah-blah-blah-blah-

(In the reflected rectangle I could see the rounded shoulders and white mane of an old woman and the serious expression of a young man.)

blah-blah-blah-blah-
blah-blah-blah-blah-
blah-blah-blah-blah-

blah-blah-blah-blah-
blah-blah-blah-blah-

("What's a mirror machine?"

"It's a machine that makes mirrors. That's how we used to make mirrors when I was a girl."

I had never heard of such a thing. "Does it still work?"

"I don't see why not. Let's see . . ."

She sat down and with her twisted fingers she opened the felt bag. I sat down beside her. She pulled out a grey plastic bottle. LIQUID SILVER, said the silver letters on it. She twisted the cap off, turned the bottle upside down, and placed the nozzle into the hole for silver atop the machine. But as she squeezed the bottle, the nozzle jumped and a heavy, round drop formed on the wood.)

blah-blah-blah-blah-
blah-blah-blah-blah-

("Here, I'll do it," I said.

The bottle, for its size, was remarkably heavy. I looked closely at the drop of silver. I teased its tense surface with the nozzle, squeezed the bottle, increasing the size of the drop, then let go, sucking it back into the bottle.)

blah-blah-blah-blah-
blah-blah-blah-blah-

("Good," said my grandmother. "Silver is expensive.")

blah-blah-blah-blah-
blah-blah-blah-blah-

(I fitted the nozzle into the hole and squeezed the bottle. A column of silver appeared at the bottom of the tube. I let it rise. When it was halfway between the MIN and MAX marks, my grandmother said, "That's enough." I squeezed a second longer and stopped.)

blah-blah-blah-blah-
blah-blah-blah-blah-

(Next she brought out of the bag a small bottle of oil and some sand. The sand was in a black, yellow and white cardboard carton. It had a drawing of a black man on a beach. He had a wide, colonized-and-happy-about-it grin on his face and wore a straw hat and clothes that were studiously tattered. NOVAK'S FINE JAMAICAN WHITE, announced the sky above him. In smaller, ornate letters around a barely decipherable coat of arms were the words "Purveyors of

Fine White Sand to His Majesty's Household.")

blah-blah-blah-blah-
blah-blah-blah-blah-
blah-blah-blah-blah-
blah-blah-blah-blah-
blah-blah-blah-blah-

("Some people would use cheap sand, sand from around here," said my grandmother. "But it makes for smoky mirrors. The best sand comes from the Caribbean.")

blah-blah-blah-blah-
blah-blah-blah-blah-
blah-blah-blah-blah-
blah-blah-blah-blah-
blah-blah-blah-blah-
blah-blah-blah-blah-

(While she poured sand through the small door, I squirted oil into the machine.)

blah-blah-blah-blah-
blah-blah-blah-blah-
blah-blah-blah-blah-
blah-blah-blah-blah-

(My grandmother sighed. "It must be fifty years since I last used this machine. Even in my time it was old and out of fashion. Now it's so much easier. You just go to a hardware store and buy an industrially manufactured, clear mirror any size or shape you want."

She paused. She was staring into midair. Her lips trembled.

"Ohhhhh, your grandfather used to rage against this machine. He who was normally such a patient man. He would jump up and want to rush out and buy a mirror that very minute. 'But we can't afford it,' I would tell him. 'We don't have the money. And the machine was given to us. We might as well use it.' He would fume. But we really didn't have the money. What do you expect? He wasn't a money man. He would often treat his patients for nothing, would even buy them the pills he prescribed when they couldn't afford them. 'Go, go for a walk, go rest, go read. I'll finish,' I'd tell him. 'Away you go!' But he would just look at me with his oh-so-beautiful eyes. Then he'd sit down beside me again and we would go on together."

She sighed tremulously.

"The long, patient hours we spent on this machine. I cannot count them." She swallowed. Her eyes were red.)

blah-blah-blah-blah-
blah-blah-blah-blah-

(On any other day I would have jostled her reminisc-
ing aside and bluntly asked her how this contraption
worked, but that day, for no particular reason, I let
her come round in her slow, anecdotal way. I eyed the
fireplace mirror again. I had noticed before that it
wasn't perfect. None of her mirrors were perfect.
They all had ridges that distorted the reflection, and
various stains and marks. But I had ascribed these
defects to age, not to handicraft origin.)

blah-blah-blah-blah-
blah-blah-blah-blah-

(She rubbed her face with her hands. She looked at the
machine. "I wonder if it still works," she said quietly.)

blah-blah-blah-blah-
blah-blah-blah-blah-
blah-blah-blah-blah-

(She extracted from the bag the most amazing thing.
It was a horn. Like for a gramophone, only smaller.
The narrow end fitted into a short, shiny brass tube
with screw threads. The other end curved and flared
out, with the edges looking like the petals of a flower.

In all decency it should have been made of plastic, but it was genuine, politically incorrect ivory, creamy white and cool and streaked with very fine black veins. It had intricate arabesque decorations on the outside, and lines that spiralled downwards on the inside. My grandmother pulled the cork from the third hole atop the machine and screwed in the horn. It could easily be rotated 360 degrees.)

blah-blah-blah-blah-
blah-blah-blah-blah-
blah-blah-blah-blah-

(The device was now fully assembled. It looked old-fashioned, peculiar and beautiful.)

blah-blah-blah-blah-
blah-blah-blah-blah-
blah-blah-blah-blah-

(Just before I could ask how it worked, she sighed.)

blah-blah-blah-blah-
blah-blah-blah-blah-
blah-blah-blah-blah-
blah-blah-blah-blah-

("Such a good man he was. I thank the Lord every day

for having put that man in my way. He took him away from me after twenty-two years of bliss, but even if I had to go through that pain ten times over, those twenty-two years would still be worth it.")

blah-blah-blah-blah-
blah-blah-blah-blah-
blah-blah-blah-blah-
blah-blah-blah-blah-
blah-blah-blah-blah-

(This was not the first time I was hearing about my grandfather. He had died of cancer of the pancreas long before I was born, and ever since I can remember he has been held up to me as the very font of goodness. He was a kind and considerate man, a devoted husband, a good father, an excellent doctor, a man of wit and culture, a lover of nature; he was wise, thoughtful, generous, sensible, decent, rational, discreet, judicious, level-headed, sober, modest, steady, virtuous; he was totally exempt from the common sins of envy, laziness, mendacity, fondness for the bottle, lechery, tardiness; he was never known to be evil-tempered, pompous, capricious, rude; and he was the possessor of magical blue eyes—they were a beacon of his goodness—of which mine were only washed-out, watered-down imitations.)

blah-blah-blah-blah-
blah-blah-blah-blah-

(For me, the man exists only in black-and-white photographs, so I cannot verify any of his attributes myself, not even the blueness of his eyes. He is a short, slightly plump man with a balding head and an oval face. He has a tiny moustache. He is neither handsome nor ugly. His other qualities are a mystery. I have often tried to extract a personality from these prints, to imagine the man beyond the frozen frames. He does look plausibly kind; perhaps a kind man of no great ambition, amply content to live his life out quietly with his family. Shy. A quiet voice, I'd think.)

blah-blah-blah-blah-
blah-blah-blah-blah-

("So how does it work?" I put in, taking advantage of a pause.

"It runs on memories."

"Sorry?"

"I said it runs on memories. On recollections, souvenirs, stories. The past."

She suffered a sudden fit of coquetry and started arranging her hair with her fingers. She cleared her throat.)

blah-blah-blah-blah-
blah-blah-blah-blah-

(Memories?)

blah-blah-blah-blah-
blah-blah-blah-blah-
blah-blah-blah-blah-
blah-blah-blah-blah-
blah-blah-blah-blah-
blah-blah-blah-blah-
blah-blah-blah-blah-

(She brought her mouth close the horn. "I," she said
clearly, "I remember . . .")

blah-blah-blah-blah-
blah-blah-blah-blah-
blah-blah-blah-blah-

(A sharp click sound. Followed by the strangest little
noise, something like a tiny locomotive starting up.
And unmistakably coming from within the machine.)

blah-blah-blah-blah-
blah-blah-blah-blah-
blah-blah-blah-blah-

blah-blah-blah-blah-
blah-blah-blah-blah-

("It still works!" she said, bringing her hands to her mouth. "Oh dear, oh dear.")

blah-blah-blah-blah-
blah-blah-blah-blah-

(That's when she started.)

blah-blah-blah-blah-
blah-blah-blah-blah-
blah-blah-blah-blah-
blah-blah-blah-blah-
blah-blah-blah-blah-
blah-blah-blah-blah-
blah-blah-blah-blah-

("I remember how I met my husband. My dear, sweet husband. It was the summer of 1928. I was sixteen and I was dressed in white. I was also wearing a straw hat, only it was too small and I was always losing it in the wind. This was in . . .")

blah-blah-blah-blah-
blah-blah-blah-blah-

blah-blah-blah-blah-
on the day he returned
home to Levis, he asked
me if he could write to me
and would I answer back.
I've kept all his letters.
Thirty-seven in a little
over a month. In the
thirty-seventh he
informed me that he was
driving down to ask for
my hand. He bought a
brand new suit just for
the occasion, and he
washed and waxed the
car. He brought Father
Bouillon along for moral
support and as a
character witness for my
parents. It was a Saturday
in early September. We
agreed to meet by the
church. I saw the car
drive up. We were both
so nervous. While
Father Bouillon
wandered off for a few

minutes, my husband, a
man of thirty but as shy
as I was, asked for my hand
in marriage. He wanted to
kiss me—and I wouldn't
have stopped him—but
there were people
walking by. I ran all the
way home and, while a
suitable hour went by,
I sat on my bed, unable to
read a line in my book,
bursting with happiness,
that Yes! Yes! Yes!
ringing in my heart. He
came at exactly four, my
handsome knight, and
Father Bouillon, who
had already mentioned
several times in glowing
terms this doctor friend
of his in letters to my
parents, spoke far too
much for a priest and
all went well. The next
spring I was seventeen
and a doctor's wife, and

six months later I was a
woman. For six months
the good man did not
touch me. Such a caring,
respectful, tender man.
What luck I had, what
a blessing he was.
I could never have found
a better man. I thank
the Lord every day for
His gift. I've had many
men propose to me since
he passed away, but no
one could replace my
sweetheart, no one. Oh
Lord, I have su-su-
suffered so much!"

She's crying.

(Far from slowing down or stopping at this interrup-
tion, the machine, with a click and a clack, kicked
into even higher gear.)

"As he was dying, he told me,

'At least I die knowing that
our children have a good
mother.' I worked myself to
the bone to bring them up
so their father would be
proud of them. It wasn't
easy, God knows. In those
days, a widow with four
children. But I managed.
I did what I had to do.
And their father would be
proud of them! They are
good children. They made
their sacrifices, too.
His example was a
blah-blah-blah-blah-
blah-blah-blah-blah-
blah-blah-blah-blah-
blah-blah-blah-blah-
blah-blah-blah-blah-
blah-blah-blah-blah-
blah-blah-blah-blah-
blah-blah-blah-blah-
blah-blah-blah-blah-
blah-blah-blah-blah-
blah-blah-blah-blah-
blah-blah-blah-blah-

This woman.

blah-blah-blah-blah-
blah-blah-blah-blah-
blah-blah-blah-blah-
blah-blah-blah-blah-
blah-blah-blah-blah-
blah-blah-blah-blah-
blah-blah-blah-blah-
blah-blah-blah-blah-
blah-blah-blah-blah-
blah-blah-blah-blah-
blah-blah-blah-blah-
blah-blah-blah-blah-
blah-blah-blah-blah-
blah-blah-blah-blah-
blah-blah-blah-blah-
blah-blah-blah-blah-
blah-blah-blah-blah-
blah-blah-blah-blah-
blah-blah-blah-blah-
blah-blah-blah-blah-
blah-blah-blah-blah-
blah-blah-blah-blah-
blah-blah-blah-blah-
blah-blah-blah-blah-
blah-blah-blah-blah-

Soft, white, wrinkled face. Green eyes but red this moment. An exasperatingly familiar face I have known since I can remember. With pouts, stares and glares that are beyond the description of words but that all of us in the family know all too well. A woman who has always been in my life.

But not for much longer, I suppose.

And what will be left of her?

blah-blah-blah-blah-
blah-blah-blah-blah-
blah-blah-blah-blah-
will you, my child?"

Her things. This
mountain of junk.
I hate all—eh?

"I'm sorry?"

"Are you deaf? I said,
Get me the photo
albums, please."

"Yes, right away."

(They are in a bookshelf near the piano. Volume after
volume. The oldest ones have wooden covers bound
with string and pages of soft, heavy black paper; the
others are the standard modern type, with adhesive
pages and clear plastic jackets. I brought over five volumes.)

"Thank you. Let's see . . .
There he is. This is
blah-blah-blah-blah-
blah-blah-blah-blah-
blah-blah-blah-blah-

(Pictures of the mystery man. A medical-school grad-
uation portrait.)

blah-blah-blah-blah-
blah-blah-blah-blah-   I hate all her junk. Gives
blah-blah-blah-blah-   me claustrophobia.
blah-blah-blah-blah-

(Sitting at the dining-room table in this house, looking at the camera.)

blah-blah-blah-blah-
blah-blah-blah-blah-   A crossed electrical wire
blah-blah-blah-blah-   would do it.
blah-blah-blah-blah-

(On a path in a wood, a cane in his right hand.)

blah-blah-blah-blah-
blah-blah-blah-blah-   Just a little fire to tidy
blah-blah-blah-blah-   things up while she's
blah-blah-blah-blah-   out.
blah-blah-blah-blah-

(On the rocky shores of the St. Lawrence, his hair
blown across his forehead by the wind.)

blah-blah-blah-blah-
blah-blah-blah-blah-   I won't lead my life this
blah-blah-blah-blah-   way, that's for sure.
blah-blah-blah-blah-

blah-blah-blah-blah-

(At the stern of a rowboat. A young woman, my grandmother, at the bow.)

blah-blah-blah-blah-
blah-blah-blah-blah-
blah-blah-blah-blah-
blah-blah-blah-blah-
blah-blah-blah-blah-
blah-blah-blah-blah-

Happiness doesn't come in dry goods of varying sizes. Happiness isn't a bulk product.

(Sitting in a garden chair, with his arms around two of his boys, one my father, a child of seven.)

blah-blah-blah-blah-
blah-blah-blah-blah-
blah-blah-blah-blah-
blah-blah-blah-blah-
blah-blah-blah-blah-

I won't exist through objects. Objects leave me cold.

(With all his children, in front of a tent.)

blah-blah-blah-blah-
blah-blah-blah-blah-
blah-blah-blah-blah-
blah-blah-blah-blah-
blah-blah-blah-blah-

Let beautiful things live in museums. Or in nature.

blah-blah-blah-blah-
blah-blah-blah-blah-

(Sitting in a sun-splashed landscape of snow, my
grandmother with a radiant smile.)

blah-blah-blah-blah-
blah-blah-blah-blah-
blah-blah-blah-blah-   I'm more preoccupied
blah-blah-blah-blah-   with furnishing my head
blah-blah-blah-blah-   than the place where I
blah-blah-blah-blah-   live. The most beautiful
blah-blah-blah-blah-   rooms I have entered
blah-blah-blah-blah-   have been empty ones.

(A frontal portrait done some weeks before his
death.)

blah-blah-blah-blah-
blah-blah-blah-blah-
blah-blah-blah-blah-   Warehouses full of light
blah-blah-blah-blah-   and dust.
blah-blah-blah-blah-   Empty attics with a view.
blah-blah-blah-blah-   Coastlines.
blah-blah-blah-blah-   Prairies.
blah-blah-blah-blah-
blah-blah-blah-blah-

(Reclining in an easy chair, covered with a blanket, asleep; the beginning of his illness?)

blah-blah-blah-blah-
blah-blah-blah-blah-
blah-blah-blah-blah- All places where my
blah-blah-blah-blah- bare, fertile humanity
blah-blah-blah-blah- has been most evident
blah-blah-blah-blah- to me.

(Sitting on a bench, looking away.)

blah-blah-blah-blah-
blah-blah-blah-blah- "Blessed are the poor in
blah-blah-blah-blah- spirit." Indeed. Blessed
blah-blah-blah-blah- in spirit are the
blah-blah-blah-blah- materially poor.
blah-blah-blah-blah-

(Group photo. Second from left.)

blah-blah-blah-blah-
blah-blah-blah-blah- I don't want the
blah-blah-blah-blah- captivity of ownership.
blah-blah-blah-blah- I want nothing but the
blah-blah-blah-blah- human, nothing else.
blah-blah-blah-blah-

blah-blah-blah-blah-
blah-blah-blah-blah-

(Full-length, standing, looking at the camera, background indistinct, hands in pockets of jacket except for thumbs.)

blah-blah-blah-blah-
blah-blah-blah-blah-
And then he died. Oh,
it breaks my heart!"

She's crying again.

(Full throttle, actually trembling with activity.)

"Why, dear Lord? Of all
people on this earth, why
my sweetheart? I don't
doubt Your all-seeing
wisdom, but why my

sweetheart? I loved that
man with all my being.
I was happy with him
for twenty-two years. For
twenty-two years it was a
pleasure to go to bed at
night, it was a pleasure to
wake up in the morning, it
was a pleasure to go about
my day. And then, then, this
unimaginable ending?
How did I survive?
I didn't. A part of me
died that day that has
never come back to life.
To my dying day I will
blah-blah-blah-blah-
blah-blah-blah-blah-
blah-blah-blah-blah-
blah-blah-blah-blah-
blah-blah-blah-blah-
blah-blah-blah-blah-
blah-blah-blah-blah-
blah-blah-blah-blah-
blah-blah-blah-blah-
blah-blah-blah-blah-
blah-blah-blah-blah-
blah-blah-blah-blah-

blah-blah-blah-blah-
blah-blah-blah-blah-
blah-blah-blah-blah-
blah-blah-blah-blah-
blah-blah-blah-blah-   I want nothing but the
blah-blah-blah-blah-   human, nothing else.
blah-blah-blah-blah-
blah-blah-blah-blah -
blah-blah-blah-blah-
blah-blah THE END!"   Eh?

(The ending was abrupt. She shouted her last two words. The machine stopped with a sharp click. A low blowing sound started.

"Is that it?" I asked.

"It should be long enough," she replied.

There was a high-pitched, grinding squeal. After a minute or so, it stopped. I heard a rolling metallic sound. Something was pushed through the machine's red velvet lips and plopped onto the table.

My eye beheld a small elliptical mirror.

"There we go," said my grandmother. She held it up and looked at herself, satisfied. "Good. No blemishes. Sometimes, for larger mirrors, you get blemishes, especially near the corners. And you have to talk for such a long time and the pieces don't always fit together perfectly. But for pocket mirrors, it does a good job."

I took hold of the mirror. It was quite warm. The back was a grey, leaden colour. I looked at my reflection.

Something caught my eye. I looked closely, angling the mirror in the light.

"It'll go away," she said. "As soon as the mirror is perfectly dry."

She was referring to the lines of print. The silver surface of the mirror was made of layer upon layer of lines of print, neatly criss-crossing at right angles.)

(I'm something of an expert on the subject now. There are generally two places in old mirrors where it is possible, with the help of a magnifying glass, to detect the lines of print: on the very edges, where the silver is thinnest; and, especially, in the stains, where oxidation sometimes brings out the print. Twice I have even managed to decipher words. The first time was in a New York antique store. I was able to tell the storekeeper that a simple but pleasing antique hand-mirror was the work of a German-speaker. In the middle of a stain I had made out the words *ganz allein*. The second time was on a subsequent visit to my grandmother. On the edge of her bedroom mirror I was able to read the syllables *ortneuf*. I had no idea what word they came from until I asked her. "St-Ray-mond-de-Portneuf," she replied. This is how I found out where my grandfather was born.

Modern mirrors are of no interest. They are indeed industrially manufactured—and clear, totally clear. There's nothing to be seen in them.)

(A late twentieth-century animist, that's what she was. Every object in her house was infused with an indwelling psyche that spoke to her of somebody or something from her long life. Her possessions were intermediaries with the deceased eternal. My grandmother lived alone in her village on the south shore of the St. Lawrence, but in fact her small house was a bustling metropolis of spirits.)

(She gave me the mirror. I still have difficulty with ownership—the apartment where I live is bare, I have few clothes, I own very little—but this pocket mirror is a prized possession. I often take it out and look at it and try to imagine all the words I so stupidly ignored.)